ECHOES ON THE BRIDGE

SOME MEMORIES DON'T BELONG TO US. BUT THEY FIND US ANYWAY

RAKESH KUMAR BHAVANI

Chapter 1: The Journey to Devotion

A Quiet Beginning

It was a serene Sunday morning in the summer of 1994. The first golden rays of sunlight stretched across the countryside, painting the vast fields in soft amber hues. Dew clung delicately to the tips of wild grass, shimmering momentarily before surrendering to the rising heat. The air smelled of earth—fresh, damp, and full of promise.

A rusted milestone stood at the turnoff, a lonely sentinel from another time, its faded arrow pointing toward "Laxmipuram 30 km." Birds perched on electric lines sang their morning hymns, their tunes weaving through the warm air, blissfully unaware of the journey unfolding beneath them. In the distance, a tractor rumbled through the sugarcane fields, its tires churning up trails of dust that hung in the golden light before fading into the breeze.

Inside a white Ambassador car that glided gently over the uneven road, a family of four embarked on a journey of faith and togetherness. Srinivas, a sturdy man in his late thirties with an ever-present sense of responsibility etched into his face, kept his eyes steady on the road. He hummed softly in sync with the cassette player spinning an old melody—a song from a time when his dreams were simpler, the world kinder.

Beside him sat Radha, his wife, draped in a mustard-yellow cotton saree. In her lap was a steel tiffin box wrapped in cloth, still warm from the morning's cooking. Her hands rested lightly on it, her fingers occasionally adjusting the folds, more out of habit than necessity. A gentle smile played on her lips as she watched the fields roll by.

Their children sat in the back seat. Fourteen-year-old Anusha, with her plaited hair tied with red ribbons, leaned toward the window, her eyes drinking in every detail of the countryside. Her brother, three-year-old Chinna, was a flurry of energy and wonder. He pressed his tiny hands and nose against the window, pointing out every bullock cart, every scarecrow, and every fluttering bird with uncontainable delight.

The scent of jasmine from Radha's hair mingled with the faint aroma of sandalwood incense tucked away in her purse, wrapping the family in a cocoon of warmth and familiarity. The rhythmic creak of the car's worn suspension became a comforting tune of its own, a lullaby that rocked them gently through time.

Toward Faith

The trip to the Veerabhadra Swamy Temple had been long overdue. For years, they had spoken of it. For years, they had promised each other it would happen. But life—with its relentless routines and unexpected hurdles—had always gotten in the way. Srinivas, employed in a demanding government post, had seldom found the luxury of time.

Today was different.

Today, devotion had taken precedence.

The highway stretched ahead, flanked by vast expanses of paddy fields that shimmered under the sun like molten gold. Here and there, the remains of forgotten festivals were etched on mud walls, faded drawings of deities and sacred symbols speaking of a village life that celebrated faith even in hardship.

Children playing on the roadside ran toward the car, waving gleefully, their laughter echoing faintly as the car sped by. Old men and women sat outside their thatched homes, some chewing betel leaves, others sipping tea from steel tumblers, their eyes lingering on the passing vehicle with curiosity and quiet understanding.

As they neared the old iron bridge at Laxmipuram, spanning a sluggish river below, Radha gripped her seat with unconscious tension. The car's tires clattered over the worn metal planks, the hollow echoes rising like chants from beneath.

"Hold tight, kids," Srinivas said playfully, glancing in the rearview mirror.

Anusha grinned, gripping Chinna's hand. He squealed in delight, unaware of anything but the thrill of the ride.

Once across, the road ascended gently into the hills, and there it was—the gopuram of the temple. It rose above the treetops, aged and silent, like a sentinel watching over the land. The sight of it stirred something deep within them, something sacred and unspoken.

Moments of Devotion

The family stepped out of the car. The gravel crunched beneath their feet as they made their way to the temple gates. They left their sandals at the entrance, and the sun-warmed stone welcomed their bare feet with the grounded intimacy of tradition.

Fragrance enveloped them—burning camphor, ghee lamps, and temple flowers. The soft murmurs of other devotees, the clinking of coins into donation boxes, and the deep, rhythmic clang of the bell formed a divine orchestra.

Inside the sanctum, the statue of Lord Veerabhadra stood fierce and unmoving. His eyes, though carved of stone, bore an intensity that pierced into the soul. He was adorned with garlands of marigold, his forehead marked with vermilion, sacred threads resting like whispers on his powerful form.

Radha closed her eyes, her lips moving in silent prayer. Srinivas placed a firm hand on Anusha's shoulder, anchoring the moment. Chinna, captivated by the priest's melodious chanting, tried to echo the Sanskrit words with childlike sincerity, drawing soft chuckles from nearby worshippers.

As they received the prasadam—a warm handful of sweet Pongal served on a leaf—they felt whole. Not because they were wealthy or free from worry, but because they were together, rooted in something far older than themselves.

An Ominous Stop

The descent from the hills was slow and calm, the temple gopuram growing smaller behind them. They had barely driven twenty minutes past Laxmipuram when Chinna tugged at Radha's saree.

"Amma... water... I'm thirsty," he said, his voice small and dry.

Srinivas scanned the empty road. Just as he was about to tell Chinna to wait, he spotted a hand pump under a grove of old banyan trees.

He slowed the car.

Radha got down with Chinna, her protective hand always resting on his back. The handle squeaked in protest as she pumped. Cool water gushed out, and Chinna drank eagerly, droplets dribbling down his chin. Anusha followed, wiping her lips with the end of her dupatta.

And then it happened.

Five men stepped out from the shadows. Their skin was darkened by sun, their expressions unreadable. One man, taller than the rest, had a jagged scar slicing across his cheek.

He spoke.

"Who gave you permission to drink here?"

Srinivas exited the car, his tone calm. "My son was thirsty. We meant no harm."

The scar-faced man took a step forward, his eyes narrowing. "This is our land. Our water. You should have asked."

The air grew heavy. Time slowed. Radha instinctively pulled Chinna behind her, while Anusha clutched her mother's pallu.

"We will leave," Srinivas said. "Please, let us go."

But reason had no place here.

A thick wooden staff swung forward and struck Srinivas on the temple. The thud echoed like a thunderclap. He crumpled to the ground, unmoving.

Radha screamed.

The men hesitated only for a moment.

"Take them," the scar-faced man ordered.

Chaos erupted. Radha clung to Chinna. Anusha tried to run but was caught. Their cries vanished into the thick trees. One of the men entered the Ambassador and drove it toward a dark river hidden beyond the fields.

With a splash, the car vanished. The ripples faded. The world fell silent.

Flashback: A Tainted Offering

A reel of memory unwound. Earlier that day, at the temple, Chinna had smiled as the priest gave him a second helping of Pongal. It was too salty, but he said nothing. Outside, as they walked back to the car, a shadow had moved past. A hand had slipped through the window. A lid turned.

Water leaked.

They returned, thinking nothing of it.

But something—or someone—had marked them.

Back to the Present

The borewell stood still again, its handle dripping water slowly, indifferently.

The banyan trees whispered nothing.

The lake, vast and unmoved, shimmered under the mid-morning sun.

And far away, in the unseen corners of fate, a new chapter waited to unfold.

Chapter 2: The Spark of Rain

A New Morning

The year was 2025. Nestled on the outskirts of a small yet vibrant town, Golden Butterfly Public School sat beside a gentle lake that shimmered beneath the morning sun. The campus was surrounded by sprawling Gul mohar trees in full bloom, their fiery red petals carpeting the earth below. The calm waters of the lake mirrored the grey stone buildings of the school, while a soft breeze occasionally sent ripples across the surface. Birds fluttered about, bathing on the shore, their songs forming a natural symphony for those walking to class.

The Lesson That Stirred Him

It was the beginning of the school day. Students walked in groups, shoes damp from dew-covered grass, their laughter ringing through the corridors. In Class 8-B, a tall, slightly lanky boy named Aryan entered the room. He held his social studies textbook close to his chest, his sharp eyes scanning the morning sky through the open windows. Today felt different. Perhaps it was the way the breeze whispered through the trees, or the heaviness in the clouds above. Something in the air stirred within him.

The school bell rang, breaking the spell of silence.

Mrs. Renu, a soft-spoken but passionate teacher in her forties, walked in with a gentle smile. She turned to the blackboard and wrote in bold white chalk: **"Resources – Water: Our Lifeline."**

Aryan leaned forward. Of all subjects, Social Studies spoke to him most. But today, this lesson on water gripped him in an unfamiliar way. It felt personal.

"Water," Mrs. Renu began, her voice calm and purposeful, "is more than a drink. It flows through our land and our lives. It brings life, shapes landscapes, and carries memories. Yet, we often take it for granted."

The room was unusually quiet. Even the backbenchers who whispered jokes during class were listening.

"Can anyone tell me," She asked, "what happens when our lakes dry up? Or when our rivers are filled with waste?"

Hands went up.

Aryan didn't raise his. He stared out at the lake near their school. He remembered the floating plastic bottles, the crumpled chip packets. In his mind, he imagined the lake empty. No fish, no ripples. Just cracked earth.

As the discussion unfolded, something shifted inside him. He imagined a future without water, without rain, without the scent of wet soil after a monsoon. The thought was terrifying.

When the bell rang to end the class, Aryan remained seated for a moment, staring at the word "Water" still lingering on the board.

The Game of Unity

Then came a new voice.

"Class 8-B!"

Coach Arvind stepped in with his signature whistle around his neck and clipboard in hand. "Time for PE. The court's ours today. Let's move!"

Cheers and groans echoed. Students packed their bags with enthusiasm or reluctance.

"Can we play cricket, sir?" someone asked.

Coach Arvind shook his head. "Basketball today. Who's playing?"

Only three boys raised their hands—Aryan, Rohan, and Suresh. Fourteen girls stood up, eager.

Coach grinned. "Alright. Three boys against fourteen girls. Let's see some magic."

The game began with energy. Aryan took centre position. His long strides and quick passes made him a natural leader. The boys, though outnumbered, dominated the court. The scoreboard read 10-0, then 16-0. The girls tried hard, their braids flying and sneakers squeaking, but the boys were swift, precise.

At halftime, Coach clapped his hands. "Time to switch it up. Aryan, you're with the girls. You five," he pointed to a group of girls, "go join the boys. Let's make it even."

Some students giggled; others exchanged surprised glances. But they followed orders.

The next half began.

This time, it was different. The teams weren't boys versus girls. It was a blend. And with that blend came unity. The ball moved faster; communication improved. Laughter echoed with every pass, every basket.

The score equalized. The tension turned into joy.

Coach blew the final whistle. "Game over. Now, what did we learn?"

Everyone stood silent, catching their breath.

Coach looked around. "It's not about boys or girls. It's about unity. That's the real victory."

Touched by Rain

As if on cue, a gust of wind swept through the court.

Then, a drop.

Then another.

Then, rain.

Students screamed and ran for shelter. Bags were held over heads, water splashed as shoes hit puddles. Laughter filled the air.

Except for Aryan.

He stood still. Head tilted to the sky. Arms at his side. Eyes closed. He let the rain fall over him. Each drop felt like a whisper, a secret from the sky. The lesson on water rang in his ears.

Then—a flash. A blinding fork of lightning cracked across the sky. It struck the basketball pole.

A loud metallic *thoom* rang out.

Aryan dropped.

Screams.

Coach Arvind dashed through the rain, heart pounding. He reached Aryan, checked his pulse, then shouted for help.

The school van became an ambulance. Aryan, soaked and limp, lay across the back seat. The van sped toward the nearby clinic.

At the hospital, doctors worked fast. Minutes felt like hours. Finally, one emerged.

"He's lucky," the doctor said. "The lightning hit the pole. The shockwave may have reached him, but no direct strike. No burns. No cardiac issue. He's just unconscious. He'll wake up soon."

Relief flooded the room. Coach Arvind sank into a chair. A nurse handed him a towel.

In the quiet room, Aryan lay still, rainwater dripping from his hair.

Outside, the rain continued.

A Deeper Awakening

As he lay unconscious, Aryan dreamed. He saw rivers forming from clouds, lakes breathing with life. He saw thirsty trees reaching up, animals gathering at waterholes, the Earth sighing with relief as monsoon winds arrived.

He saw the lake behind his school, clean and clear. And then he saw it dry, barren, forgotten. He reached out, but the lake faded.

He awoke with a gasp.

Beside him, his mother held his hand.

"Maa?"

"Yes, son. I'm here. I never left."

Aryan looked around, then whispered, "I saw the sky. It... knew."

She wiped his forehead. "Don't talk now. Just rest."

But Aryan could not sleep. The dream clung to him like the rain on his skin.

Ripples at School

The next morning, the school buzzed with stories. Aryan was a hero. A survivor. Some said he had superpowers now. Others whispered he had spoken to the rain.

Mrs. Renu entered Class 8-B. Her eyes were moist. She looked at her students and asked, "Do you know what true courage is?"

Silence.

She answered, "It's standing still in the storm. Not from recklessness. But because your heart hears something others don't."

Every student thought of Aryan.

Three days later, Aryan returned. He was quieter. Thoughtful.

During lunch, he walked to the lake. The banyan tree gave him shade. He opened his notebook and wrote:

"Water doesn't shout to be powerful. It flows. It waits. It gives. It protects more than we know."

Something had shifted. Aryan hadn't just learned about water. He had been chosen by it.

And now, every time it rained, he listened.

Not with fear.

But with gratitude.

Chapter 3: The Road to Laxmipuram

A Day Unlike Any Other

The next morning, the sun rose lazily over Golden Butterfly Public School, casting a warm, golden hue across the dew-kissed playground. A soft mist clung to the gates and slowly lifted as students began to arrive, their excitement buzzing in the cool morning air. But today wasn't just any school day. Today, the children carried something different in their backpacks—not just textbooks, but home-packed lunches, rolled-up floor mats, chessboards, sketchbooks, and snack pouches. The air was thick with anticipation.

The long-awaited school excursion was finally happening.

The students of Class 8, along with a few other middle schoolers, were heading to Laxmipuram—a scenic town known for its age-old temples, misty groves, and its deep, enduring connection with water and forest ecosystems. It wasn't just a sightseeing trip. It was an educational journey—to observe, learn, and connect with the roots of nature.

Aboard the Rolling Classroom

Aryan stood beside the school bus, quiet but watchful. Still recovering from the lightning scare that had made him something of a legend on campus, he clutched a magnetic chessboard in one hand and a neatly packed lunch in the other. Rohan and Suresh, his closest friends, were already inside.

"Come on, Aryan! Window seat's ours today!" Rohan called from the back.

With a soft smile, Aryan climbed aboard. The bus was newer than most—a modern, air-conditioned vehicle with plush seats and large windows that turned the countryside into a movie screen. Inside, the chaos had already begun. Some students were playing antakshari, others diving into animated games of dumb charades. A group of girls had started an impromptu art contest, while a few boys huddled around a phone, giggling at old cartoons.

Near the front, teachers handed out printed schedules and whispered final checklists. Coach Arvind gave a mini safety speech, his whistle dangling from his neck like a badge of authority.

With a gentle purr, the engine came to life, and the bus
began to roll.

Moments on the Move

Aryan settled into his seat and unfolded his magnetic
chessboard on his lap. The tiny plastic pieces clicked into
place as he and Suresh played a casual match. Outside, the
bustling town slowly gave way to open fields and long
stretches of road. Yellow mustard flowers waved from
both sides as if blessing their journey.

About forty minutes in, the bus slowed. A road sign
flashed by: "Laxmipuram Temple – 25 KM."

The bus turned off the main highway and onto a
countryside path lined with mango groves and patches of
dense shrubbery. It was here, among the moving greens,
that something strange happened.

The Flash

A sudden burst of light outside made Aryan squint. It
wasn't sunlight—it had a silvery shimmer, almost like a
reflection from another time. Instinctively, he closed his
eyes. But what met him behind those closed lids was not
darkness.

A bridge. Rusty. Cracked. Draped in vines. Shrouded in
mist.

It was vivid—too vivid. A vision, a memory, a premonition? He couldn't say. But it shook him.

He opened his eyes. The landscape remained unchanged—only fields, farmers, and the occasional scarecrow. But the image had etched itself deep in his mind.

"You, okay?" Suresh asked, nudging his pawn forward.

Aryan nodded slowly. "Yeah... just spaced out."

The Rusted Memory

They soon passed a small village where tiled-roof homes clung to winding lanes, and barefoot children waved from a wall. Aryan barely noticed. His eyes remained on the road ahead—where distant shapes began to form.

And then it appeared.

The bridge.

It was exactly as he had seen it. Rusted iron beams. Thick vines. Birds fluttering through gaps in the structure. An eerie silence wrapped around it.

Gasps filled the bus as students pressed to the windows.

"Look at that old bridge!" someone shouted.

But the bus didn't cross it. Instead, it took the newer cement bridge constructed parallel to the old one. Wide, safe, and silent.

The vehicle slowed to a near halt at the middle.

"Everyone, observe from your seats," announced Mrs. Renu. "We're witnessing both man-made and natural interaction. Now—who can tell me a resource that may vanish if not protected?"

A girl up front responded, "Water!"

"Correct," Renu nodded. "And what man-made activity consumes natural resources quickly?"

Aryan, his eyes still fixed on the rusted bridge, whispered, "Iron mining."

She turned to him. "Well said. Iron makes these bridges, but its extraction scars the earth. Every structure we build must respect the nature it borrows from."

Students applauded. But Aryan didn't smile. A strange heaviness pressed on his chest.

A Fading View

The bus moved on. Aryan's hands felt cold. He wiped his forehead, surprised by its warmth.

"Ma'am," he whispered. "I don't feel good."

Mrs. Renu approached. His face was pale. She handed him a small motion-sickness tablet and a bottle of water.

"Take this and rest, Aryan," she said gently.

He nodded and leaned on Suresh's shoulder, chessboard still in hand. His eyes fluttered closed.

But instead of slipping into peaceful sleep, he tumbled into something deeper.

The Dream of the Bridge

He stood at the edge of the same rusty bridge. This time, it wasn't abandoned.

A figure was there.

Far off, near the middle—a girl. Her silhouette was faint, almost see-through. Her hair flowed with the breeze, and she seemed to be staring at the river below.

Aryan stepped forward, unable to speak, drawn by something he couldn't explain. Each footstep echoed against the rusted planks. The wind howled louder.

The girl turned.

But her face—

It was blurred.

Before he could move closer, the sky turned crimson. A loud thunderclap shook the bridge.

And then—he fell.

The Descent

Aryan's body jerked slightly in real life. His fingers tightened over the chessboard. But in his dream, he was underwater, sinking slowly. Light from above shimmered, dancing on the surface. Shapes floated around him—a drawing, a glass of rose milk, a cherry drifting upward.

He reached for them.

Whispers of the Unknown

Just before everything turned dark, he heard a whisper. A breath. Faint, almost drowned by the murmur of water.

It wasn't a name—at least, not one he could grasp. It slipped past his consciousness like wind over still water, refusing to be remembered.

His eyes flickered open for a second in the real world, but his mind was still caught in the dream. A chill ran down his spine. The name repeated in his thoughts, uninvited and unfamiliar.

The bus rolled on toward Laxmipuram. Laughter and chatter returned as the stop neared. But Aryan remained asleep, his brow gently furrowed.

A new chapter had begun.

Chapter 4: The Bridge

A Return to Wakefulness

The bus continued to move steadily along the winding road, cutting through the fading orange of the evening light. Aryan stirred in his sleep. His eyelids fluttered open slowly, and he blinked twice to adjust to the dimming interior light of the bus.

But something was off.

Suresh was no longer beside him.

Instead, a girl—one he didn't recognize—was sitting next to him, looking out the window in complete silence. Her hair was neatly tied in a long braid, and she wore a soft lavender kurta with glass bangles gently clinking against each other as the bus jolted. Aryan's body tensed. He sat up suddenly and accidentally hit his forehead on the metal carriage rack above the seat.

"Ow!" he muttered, wincing in pain and clutching his head.

"Amma?" he said out loud instinctively, his voice laced with fear and confusion.

The movement caught the attention of his teacher, Mrs. Renu, who rushed over.

"Aryan... Aryan! Wake up, dear."

His eyes blinked again—and this time, it was Suresh who was beside him, asleep with his head leaning against the window. The strange girl was gone.

It had been a dream. Or… something that felt far more vivid than any dream should.

As Aryan rubbed his forehead, still disoriented, the scenery outside had changed dramatically. They were deep within the forest path now, surrounded by tall trees and occasional glimpses of the river running parallel to the road. The light was golden orange—dusk was approaching.

What Was Missed

"Have we… reached the temple yet?" he asked softly.

His teacher chuckled and nodded. "Oh, Aryan… you were fast asleep the whole time! We visited the temple, explored the forest trail, saw the lake, and even dipped our hands in the river. You missed all of it!"

Some of the students nearby laughed, not cruelly, but teasingly. Aryan's heart sank. The tears welled up quietly in his eyes and spilled onto his cheeks without warning. He had been waiting for this trip. The temple. The lake. The forest. He had longed to feel it all… and yet, it had all passed him by while he was lost in sleep.

Seeing this, Mrs. Renu's expression softened immediately. She motioned to Suresh to switch seats and gently sat beside Aryan. She wiped away the tears from his cheek.

"It's okay, beta. Don't feel bad," she said softly. "We'll take you there again. I promise."

But the laughter from the back continued to echo, until Coach Arvind, who hadn't spoken all day, let out a sharp whistle that pierced through the bus. The noise dropped into pin-drop silence.

That single whistle said everything.

The Unexpected Stop

And then, surprisingly, the bus slowed to a halt.

Students peered curiously out the window.

"Why did we stop?" someone asked.

Up ahead, a large herd of sheep were crossing the narrow road, moving toward the left where the river shimmered in the sunset glow. The driver stood up and pointed.

"Let them pass. Look—how beautiful they are... headed to the river to drink water."

Aryan, still sniffling, looked outside. The scene was almost magical. Dozens of sheep, white and brown, crossed gently across the road. Beyond them, the river gleamed like glass, reflecting the orange rays of the setting sun. He stared at it for a long moment, soaking in its serenity. His heart felt heavier and lighter at once.

"Can I see the temple from the back window?" he asked suddenly.

Mrs. Renu nodded. "Go ahead, dear. I'll come with you."

Together they walked toward the back of the bus. Aryan squinted through the large rear window, scanning the landscape behind them. No temple was clearly visible—it had faded into the distance.

But then, just as he was about to turn back, something caught his eye.

A hand-pump borewell stood near the base of a banyan tree, its curved metal frame glinting faintly in the twilight.

And beside it...

The girl from his dream.

Standing silently. Her lavender kurta. Her braid. The same expressionless eyes.

Aryan froze.

As the bus began to roll forward again, the borewell and the girl grew smaller and smaller, finally melting into the landscape like mist dissolving into the sky.

He stood frozen for a moment longer before returning to his seat.

Across the Bridge

As they continued forward, the road straightened, and the bus began to approach the bridge—the very bridge where Aryan had first seen the strange vision.

"Aryan, Aryan," Mrs. Renu called softly. "Come here. You'll want to see this."

He followed her to the front of the bus. Coach Arvind stood beside the driver and offered a hand to help Aryan forward.

From the front windshield, the bridge came into view.

And something else too.

An old-fashioned white Benz car was parked on the bridge with its fog lights and parking lights still on. The bus slowed again.

Beside the car stood a man in a maroon shirt and white pants, wearing thick gold chains around his neck and fingers heavy with gold rings. He had a large moustache, and as he turned slightly while speaking into his mobile phone, Aryan's eyes caught a glimpse of a long scar across the man's face.

His stomach churned.

Something about the man unsettled Aryan deeply. His thick gold chains, the way he stood with silent authority—and most of all, the long scar that ran across his face. Aryan had never seen him before, but the sight sent a chill through his bones.

He stumbled back into the aisle and clutched Mrs. Renu's arm, shaking violently. "It's him... the man... something about him... it's frightening."

She wrapped an arm around him. "It's alright, Aryan. He's just a traveller. Don't be afraid."

The drivers exchanged brief words about a punctured tire. The man barely acknowledged them—still deep in his phone conversation.

But Aryan couldn't take his eyes off the man's face.

The bus slowly passed the car, inching over the old rusty bridge. Every student was peeking from the windows, fascinated by the strange car, the man, and the setting sun casting fire-coloured shadows over the structure.

Into the Night

As they cleared the bridge, the interior lights of the bus dimmed. Slowly, one by one, students drifted into naps, lulled by the movement of the bus and the day's fatigue.

Aryan sat silently by the window, his body curled slightly, his mind racing.

His teacher glanced at him and gently placed a hand on his shoulder. He didn't respond. He had fallen asleep again—this time not from exhaustion, but from a strange heaviness.

The bus finally arrived back at school after nightfall. Parents had begun lining up to collect their children. The staff moved through the rows, waking up students and handing them over one by one.

When Mrs. Renu reached Aryan, she paused.

His forehead was burning with fever.

She placed her hand gently on his cheeks. He was shivering.

"Coach, please help," she said. "He's burning up."

Coach Arvind quickly carried the boy in his arms and led him to the waiting school van.

"We'll take him to the hospital. Something's not right," the teacher said urgently.

The headlights of the van cut through the dark as it pulled away.

In the distance, across the now-quiet street, the wind picked up again.

And somewhere—far beyond—the sound of a lone hand-pump echoed faintly through the night.

Chapter 5: The Drawing

Three Days Later

Three days passed. Aryan lay resting under the soft white sheets of the hospital bed. Machines beeped quietly in the background while sunlight filtered through pale blue curtains, casting faint shadows on the tiled floor. His mother dozed in the chair beside him, and his father, standing by the window, stared at the trees lining the hospital grounds.

Suddenly, Aryan stirred. His eyes fluttered open, slowly adjusting to the sterile white of the ceiling above.

"Amma..." he said weakly.

His mother jumped up. "Aryan! You're awake!"

His father rushed over, overwhelmed with emotion. Aryan looked at both of them, then sat up slowly, though his limbs still ached.

"I want to go to Laxmipuram," he said softly, his voice almost a whisper. "I want to see the temple... the river... the lake... and the forest. I want to see it for real."

His parents looked at each other. His father knelt beside the bed, cupping Aryan's hand in his.

"You will, son. But first, you must recover fully. We'll go together... soon."

Aryan nodded, but his mind was already elsewhere.

A Strange Return to School

The next day, Aryan returned to school.

The morning should have been normal. But as soon as he stepped through the gates, something felt off. A crowd of parents huddled near the administrative block, many of them talking frantically. Policemen stood around the corridor, questioning teachers and ushering students to different rooms. The entire campus buzzed with unease.

Aryan's footsteps slowed.

He spotted his teacher, Mrs. Renu, near the office room. Before he could speak, she saw him and quickly approached. "Aryan... stay back for a moment, alright?"

He was stunned. "What's happening, ma'am?"

She hesitated. "Just... wait here."

Confused and concerned, Aryan walked toward Rohan, who sat on a bench outside the office room, chewing his nails nervously.

"What's going on?" Aryan whispered. "Why are there so many police and parents here?"

Rohan looked up and blinked. "You... you don't know?"

Aryan shook his head.

Rohan leaned in. "Five girls from our class… the ones who swapped with us during the basketball game… they're missing. No one's seen them for four days now."

Aryan's heart skipped.

"They went missing four days ago. Same evening of the trip. Their parents thought they'd come home late… but they never arrived. Everyone's panicking. The school's being questioned. The coach was taken to the police station. Now they're talking to each teacher and student from the trip."

Aryan's hands trembled. "But… but I was in the hospital…"

Just then, a parent's voice shouted. "He wasn't here! This boy! He was missing too!"

Heads turned. Parents surged forward, pointing fingers and yelling questions.

"Where were you, boy?" "Did you see them?" "Were you with the girls?" "Did anything strange happen?"

Aryan shrank back. The noise overwhelmed him. His breathing quickened.

"Enough!" shouted Mrs. Renu, stepping in front of Aryan. "He was hospitalized since the day of the tour! He fainted due to lightning exposure! He has no idea what's happening!"

She turned and motioned to the security staff. "Please escort him to the classroom."

Aryan, though taller than his teacher, stayed close behind her, shielding himself from the angry crowd. Rohan followed, and the security guards flanked them as they walked through the long corridor toward their classroom.

The Art Period

In Class 8-B, the atmosphere was tense. Students sat quietly, heads down. The usual chatter and giggles were gone. Everyone sensed that something terrible had happened, something bigger than any of them could understand.

It was the art period.

The teacher, Mr. Ravi, a calm and imaginative man in his 30s, entered the room holding a thick sketchbook and a bundle of pencils.

"Today," he said, his voice gentle but firm, "we're not doing textbook art. I want you to draw what's in your mind. Anything. A memory, a dream, a moment. Something that stayed with you."

Students slowly pulled out sketchbooks and began scribbling with coloured pencils, sketch pens, crayons. Bright colours filled the room—scenes of the forest, the river, even the temple's gopuram.

Aryan sat silently at his desk.

His hand reached for a black pencil.

No colours. Just black.

He began to draw.

Line by line, stroke by stroke. His mind filled in images his words never could.

A bridge—long, rusted, stretching into the fog.

A borewell, crooked and shadowed under a banyan tree.

A girl in a lavender kurta with a braid, standing still.

A boy inside a bus, looking out through a wide glass window, watching her fade away.

When he was done, he just stared at it.

Simple. Black lines. But the feeling—cold and unsettling—seeped through the paper.

The class was called to present their art.

One by one, students showed their colourful landscapes, their temples, animals, and forests.

Then it was Aryan's turn.

As he walked toward the front of the class, students formed a line to show their work to Mr. Ravi, who was carefully reviewing each piece. Aryan stood to the side, waiting. At that moment, Ms. Ramya, another art teacher, entered the classroom quietly, checking the students' work and speaking softly to a few near the back.

Aryan, unsure whether to wait or go back to his seat, simply placed his sketch on the desk at the front and walked away.

Behind the Staffroom Doors

Ten minutes later, chaos moved quietly behind the scenes.

Ms. Ramya picked it up, her eyes catching the black strokes almost immediately. Something about the image held her gaze. Without saying anything to Mr. Ravi, who was still busy reviewing other drawings, she gently tucked the sketch under her notebook and stepped out of the room.

In the staff room, Ms. Ramya showed the drawing to Mrs. Renu, who gasped, her hand flying to her mouth. Without wasting a second, they made their way straight to the principal's office.

Inside the principal's office, the atmosphere grew tense. The sketch was placed on the table. No one spoke for a while.

The principal, Mrs. Renu, and a few teachers leaned over it.

The principal's face hardened. She looked at Ms. Ramya and said, "Please call Aryan's parents. Do it now."

The art teacher nodded and walked quickly toward Class 8-B.

Chapter 6: The Painted Truth

The Gathering Storm

Aryan sat inside the small office room of the school, where the air was cool and still. The faint scent of chalk and old wooden furniture lingered in the air. A stack of files sat untouched in one corner, and a slow-moving fan creaked above them. Despite the tense atmosphere in the school, inside this room, there was a strange silence.

Opposite Aryan sat his teacher, Mrs. Renu, gently moving pawns across a magnetic chessboard. Chess always calmed Aryan. The strategy, the silence between moves—it helped him focus. The boy leaned forward, eyes fixated, and moved his knight into a clever position.

"Check," he whispered.

Mrs. Renu smiled faintly, but her mind wasn't in the game. It was outside, in the waiting hall, where chaos brewed.

The Drawing in Question

In the main corridor, the principal sat surrounded by a police officer and a growing group of anxious parents. Questions buzzed like bees around a hive.

"They were just kids! How could five girls go missing under your watch?" one parent shouted.

Another added, "And now this drawing? How can a boy draw them days after they vanished?"

Just then, Aryan's parents arrived at the school gates. They hurried through the hallway, visibly confused. The moment they stepped into the crowd, a sea of questions surged toward them.

"You're Aryan's parents?"
"Where is your son?"
"Did he say anything to you?"
"How did he know where the girls were?"

Aryan's mother looked stunned. "What? What are you talking about?"

The police officer stepped forward, raising a hand. "Please calm down, everyone. Let them speak."

The officer turned to Aryan's father. "Sir, your son was hospitalized after the school trip, correct?"

"Yes, for three days. Then he was resting at home. He just returned to school today," the father replied.

The officer nodded and pulled out Aryan's now-infamous drawing. "Has your son drawn anything like this at home? Did he speak of this girl... this bridge... or this borewell?"

Aryan's mother stared at the sketch, her eyes lingering on the dark, eerie lines. "No... he didn't draw anything. He did mention he wanted to go to Laxmipuram, to see the temple, the river, the forest. But that was all."

The principal, who had been quiet, now stepped forward. "We believe the image he drew includes details of the location where the five missing girls were last seen. His drawing shows the same area we visited during the trip, but there's something strange..."

She traced her finger over the faint figures near the tree. Five silhouettes, barely outlined, near the borewell and edge of the forest.

The police officer took a breath and said, "Bring Aryan here. Now."

Aryan Questioned

Back in the office, Aryan was quietly repositioning the rook. His teacher received the message and closed the chessboard gently.

"Come with me, Aryan. The principal wants to speak to you."

He followed without question.

When they entered the hallway, everyone turned. His parents walked quickly to him, both worried and protective. They embraced him tightly.

"Don't worry," his father whispered. "Just answer honestly."

A police officer stepped forward and knelt beside Aryan.

"Aryan, can you tell me about this picture?" he asked, holding the sketch.

Aryan glanced at it and frowned. "That's not how I drew it..."

The officer raised his brow. "Explain."

"I drew the bridge. The white car with lights. The river. The lake. The girl by the borewell. But not... the five girls. I never drew them. I didn't even think of them."

He looked at the picture again, fear creeping into his eyes. "Why are they there now?"

The officer studied Aryan's face, measuring his reaction.

"Do you think the girls could be near that location?"

"I... I don't know," Aryan said honestly. "We passed the borewell on the trip. That's where I saw the girl. I don't remember anything about the others."

The officer turned to his colleague. "We have enough. Send a team out now."

Mobilizing the Search

While Aryan was escorted back to the room with his parents, a police search team was mobilized. Maps were unfolded on the principal's desk. Officers marked the temple, the old bridge, the surrounding forest paths, and the location of the borewell as drawn in Aryan's sketch.

That evening, under fading light, four jeeps headed out to Laxmipuram.

Back at the school, Aryan sat quietly while his mother gently stroked his hair. His father kept checking his phone, watching the minutes pass like hours.

The school had emptied out. Only the principal, a few staff, and two police officers remained.

Ms. Ramya walked into the room with a fresh drawing pad. "Aryan," she said softly, "would you mind trying something again?"

Aryan looked up. "Draw?"

"Yes. Anything that comes to your mind. Don't think. Just draw."

Aryan nodded and began sketching slowly, using only black again. The room was silent.

After 10 minutes, he paused and turned the page.

This time, the image was of the same borewell... but the girl had her hand raised, pointing toward the trees behind her.

Ms. Ramya, who had quietly entered behind them, took the sketch and hurried to the principal's office once again.

Into the Forest

Meanwhile, in the forest near Laxmipuram, search teams scoured the woods with flashlights and dogs. They passed the temple and reached the bridge. Everything in Aryan's sketch matched the real landscape.

Finally, one of the officers radioed in.

"We found the borewell. There's a trail behind it. Looks like it hasn't been used in years."

Within minutes, they followed the path. About 200 meters in, they discovered remnants of torn cloth, a broken bracelet, and a school bag with a nametag.

The radio crackled again: "Confirming—belongings found. Proceeding deeper."

Back in the school, Aryan watched as Ms. Ramya and the police officers returned, their faces tense. The radio continued updating them as officers searched deeper into the woods.

At midnight, a final message came in: "Search continues. No contact yet."

A heavy silence filled the room.

Aryan looked at his parents. His father gripped his hand tightly. His mother wept.

Unanswered Questions

The search continued through the night, but the forest remained silent. No further clues were found beyond the scattered belongings. Officers radioed back updates every hour, but none of them brought the answers anyone was hoping for. All of them told the same story: they had been separated after the trip and had wandered off unknowingly, lured by something... or someone.

They remembered the borewell. The tree. The river. But nothing after that.

One of them, barely awake, whispered: "There was a girl... she kept walking ahead. We followed. Then everything went dark."

Aryan sat beside the window, watching the first light of dawn.

He picked up the last sketch. The girl still pointed toward the woods. Her expression now seemed less blank... more knowing.

Who was she? And why had only he seen her?

The forest had given some answers. But it had also opened the door to deeper mysteries.

Chapter 7: The Map

The Storm Approaches

The clock ticked slowly inside the principal's office. Outside, rain clouds loomed in the distance, casting long shadows across the school corridors. The fluorescent lights inside flickered slightly, reacting to the change in air pressure as thunder echoed somewhere far beyond the horizon.

The phone on the principal's desk rang. She picked it up immediately, her tone shifting from tired to alert. Her face tensed as she listened to the voice on the other end.

"Yes? Go ahead…"

It was a call from the forest search team. The voice crackled with static.

"We've gone deeper into the forest. No signs yet. Still searching. The trail ends at the edge of the river. We're splitting into two teams to search the western and southern edges."

The principal nodded; her voice low. "Keep us informed."

She hung up slowly, glancing toward the hallway where parents and teachers waited with frayed nerves.

A Friend Arrives

Just then, there was a knock at the door. Rohan stood outside, peeking in with a hesitant expression.

"Ma'am, may I come in?"

The principal waved him in.

Rohan entered, scanning the room until his eyes met Aryan's. He smiled slightly and walked toward him.

"Hey, you, okay?"

Aryan nodded, still feeling the fog of questions and silence surrounding him. They stood there for a few seconds in mutual quiet, not needing to say much. Sometimes friends don't need explanations.

Trying to change the subject, Rohan said, "You remember the topic we were discussing before the trip? Resources and landscapes. You know... lakes, rivers, forest reserves?"

Aryan's eyes moved, and he nodded again.

"I was thinking," Rohan continued, "if we could just look at the area from a map, maybe we'd understand better how the forest spreads out. It might help us see something the police haven't yet."

Aryan blinked. "But we don't have our phones."

"Right."

Then Aryan looked up suddenly. "Wait here."

Borrowed Time

Aryan walked over to his father, who was seated in the hallway with worry written across his face. He was scrolling through messages and missed calls from relatives who had caught glimpses of the news spreading on local channels.

"Nanna... can I borrow your phone? Just for a minute. I want to see the map of Laxmipuram."

His father hesitated, confused. "Aryan... this isn't the time."

"Please. I just want to check something. It's important."

There was something in Aryan's tone that made his father pause. After a brief moment, he nodded and handed the phone over. "Sit right here. I'll be watching."

Aryan returned to Rohan, phone in hand. The boys sat side by side on the wooden bench just outside the principal's office. The hallway around them had grown quieter. Everyone's energy was running out.

Aryan unlocked the phone and opened Google Maps. The familiar satellite view loaded. The school grounds appeared first, and Aryan typed in "Golden Butterfly

Public School."

The screen sharpened. Their rectangular classrooms, the long corridor, the open grass field—all came into view.

"Look at this," Rohan whispered. "That's our building. And that's the basketball court."

Aryan pinched the screen, zooming out slowly. "There's the main road. And the highway..."

He typed "Laxmipuram." The map shifted and jumped.

"There."

They saw it clearly. The cluster of temple roofs, the bridge beside the slow-moving river, the old and the new roads running parallel.

Retracing the Path

"Look," Aryan pointed, "here's where we took the turn. This is the trail through the forest. And that's the river. It's huge."

Zooming in slowly, they could see the textures of the terrain—dense trees, narrow paths, clearings, and shadows that hinted at elevation. Aryan's heart beat faster.

"And that," he whispered, pointing to a dark patch near a curve, "is the borewell."

"How can, you be sure?" asked Rohan.

"Because I remember the tree next to it. It had thick roots wrapped around the base. It was right there."

Rohan leaned closer. "That's exactly where the bus stopped."

Aryan's fingers moved, tracing the path of the search teams as if drawing invisible lines. He zoomed further into the river's edge.

And then, something caught his eye.

The White Smudge

"What is that?" he muttered.

"Where?" Rohan leaned even closer.

"There." Aryan tapped the screen.

Near the northern rim of the river, partially shielded by the shadows of the trees, was a white shape. It was unlike the rocks nearby. It was too smooth. Too rounded.

"It doesn't look natural," Aryan said.

"Maybe it's a boat?" Rohan guessed.

"Or a structure. But why would it be there?"

Aryan's fingers moved to zoom in further.

But before he could see more, a voice called from behind.

"Rohan!"

It was Mrs. Renu.

Rohan stood up. "I'll be right back," he said. "Don't close it."

Aryan nodded.

Rohan jogged away as Aryan sat there, phone still glowing. He stared at the shape. It felt… wrong. It didn't belong. His chest tightened. His thumb hovered over the screen.

Called In

Then the hallway shifted again.

The principal stepped out of her office.

"Aryan. Mr. and Mrs. Kumar. Please come inside."

His father reached out and gently took the phone back. "Come, son."

Aryan followed them inside. The door clicked softly behind them.

On the bench, the phone screen dimmed. The image of the white smudge blurred and faded.

And outside, the Storm

Thunder rolled again, closer now. The wind swept through the trees outside the school, bending their branches toward the earth. Rain began to tap on the windows.

And hundreds of kilometres away, in Laxmipuram, the same wind rustled the leaves around the river.

The white shape sat still, unmoving.

Waiting.

Chapter 8: The Return to Laxmipuram

The Arrival of Authority

The air inside the principal's office had shifted. The tension that had hovered like a heavy cloud over the past few days was replaced—if only slightly—with a new sense of purpose. The senior IPS officer had arrived.

He was a man in his late fifties, short but with a posture that radiated authority and calm. His neatly combed silver hair, sharp eyes, and creased uniform—even though he had just landed from a flight—spoke of decades of experience. When he entered the room, the atmosphere changed. Teachers, parents, even the junior officers instinctively straightened up.

After hearing the full case briefing, he turned toward Aryan's parents. His voice wasn't loud, but it carried weight.

"We need your son's help. Aryan has seen something we haven't. And it's possible his presence could unlock the next step in this search."

Aryan's father looked uneasy. "Sir, he's just a child. He's been through so much. He fainted, he had a fever, and now this pressure..."

The IPS officer stepped closer, his tone softer. "I understand. But I wouldn't ask if it wasn't important. And I'll personally ensure his safety."

There was something in the old man's eyes. A knowing seriousness. Not just that of a policeman, but of a father too. Aryan's father looked at his wife, who gave a quiet nod. Aryan stood nearby, watching. He wasn't afraid. In fact, he looked... curious. Almost eager.

Without another word, the father agreed.

The Convoy Sets Out

By mid-morning, the group had boarded a convoy of vehicles headed for Laxmipuram. There were two police jeeps with search equipment and trained officers. Another van held the coach, the teacher, and three parents of the missing girls. The last, most sophisticated vehicle was reserved for Aryan's family and the IPS officer.

It was a large SUV—black, polished, with tinted windows and reinforced doors. Inside, it had padded seats, a small screen with live GPS tracking, a backup radio system, and a compact cabinet for gear and case files.

Aryan sat near the window, his father beside him. His mother sat in the back row with one of the officer's assistants. The IPS officer rode in the front seat, calmly reviewing a folder of maps, satellite images, and reports.

As they neared a roundabout, the IPS officer said quietly to the driver, "Turn off here. I need to stop home for five minutes. I need my field notes and sidearm."

The driver nodded and took a turn down a private lane. Aryan looked out and saw a tall black gate slowly opening. The van turned into a sprawling property.

The Officer's Residence

The IPS officer's house was large, but simple in tone. It wasn't flashy or gold-plated. It stood on a gentle rise with polished stone walls, wide balconies, and antique-style railings. There were at least four cars parked—two SUVs, one old Ambassador, and a compact vintage Fiat.

The front lawn was large and clean, with potted trees, trimmed hedges, and an old swing chair made of wood and iron gently swaying in the breeze. A tiled pathway curved toward a side garage. Two large dogs watched silently from a distance.

House staff moved quietly across the grounds. Two men were washing the cars. A maid stood by the front door. Another elderly helper—slightly hunched, with greying hair and thin limbs—stood just inside the doorway. It was Shankar Kaka.

The IPS officer stepped out of the SUV and turned to the group. "Would anyone like something to drink?"

Aryan's father hesitated, then said, "A cup of tea would be good."

"I'll have the same," added Aryan's mother.

Aryan chimed in, almost on instinct. "Ice rose milk. With cherry on top!"

There was a pause.

The IPS officer turned slowly. Aryan's parents turned too. The driver looked up through the mirror.

Shankar Kaka, who had remained still, flinched.

Aryan didn't notice. He was smiling faintly.

The IPS officer nodded. "Kaka, two ginger teas, and rose milk for the young one. With cherry."

Aryan's parents looked puzzled, but said nothing. Aryan, meanwhile, was fidgeting in his seat.

"I need to use the restroom," he said.

His father nodded. The driver stepped out and opened the door. Aryan stepped confidently through the gate, smiled at the maid, and nodded politely to Shankar Kaka.

Inside the Officer's Home

The house was cool and spacious. The floors were marble, the walls clean and lined with framed photographs—black-and-white portraits, award ceremonies, a family group with the same officer in a younger avatar. One photo showed him shaking hands with the President of India.

Aryan didn't stare long. He located the bathroom, used it quickly, then wandered briefly through the drawing room. The wooden swing outside the window creaked softly in the wind.

He turned back and made his way outside just as Shankar Kaka appeared carrying a tray.

The Moment

On the tray were two stainless steel tumblers in curved brass holders, filled with steaming ginger tea. Between them sat a frosted glass of pink rose milk, crowned with thick cream and a single red cherry. A small steel plate held square salt biscuits, neatly arranged.

The IPS officer stepped outside with his files and tablet bag, now fully suited in his uniform. He accepted one tea tumbler and passed the other to Aryan's father. Aryan's mother was handed hers, and finally, Aryan took the rose milk glass.

As he took it into his hands, he smiled gently. "Thank you, Shankar Kaka."

Everyone froze.

Shankar Kaka's expression shifted. His hands trembled slightly.

Aryan's parents turned to each other with wide eyes.

The IPS officer looked directly at Aryan. "Have you been here before?"

Aryan shook his head, taking a small sip. "No... it's just nice. And familiar."

He carefully picked out the cherry with two fingers, placed it between his lips, and finished the drink. Then he handed the glass back to Kaka.

"Thank you," he said again.

The Departure

No one spoke as they boarded the vehicle.

Even the normally composed IPS officer looked uncertain, his gaze lingering on Aryan's face in the rearview mirror.

The gates opened slowly, creaking on their hinges. The SUV pulled away.

Back at the porch, Shankar Kaka stood motionless.

The officer's maid turned to him and whispered, "How did he know your name?"

But Kaka didn't answer.

He only watched the SUV disappear down the road.

Chapter 9: The Threat Revealed

The Call That Changed Direction

The vehicle carrying Aryan, his parents, and the IPS officer sped forward to rejoin the convoy. Dust rose from the wheels as the black SUV cut through a highway bend, sunlight flickering through tree branches as they passed. Inside, the mood was quiet but alert. Aryan watched the horizon, his fingers resting on the edge of the window. The IPS officer, composed as ever, sat reviewing satellite maps on his tablet, murmuring soft notes to himself.

In the lead van, the atmosphere suddenly shifted. Mrs. Renu was adjusting her bag when a phone vibrated loudly, cutting through the low hum of road noise. It belonged to Ashok, father of Asha—one of the missing girls. He hesitated at the sight of the unknown number, then answered.

Silence.

Then a voice, cold and emotionless: "Turn around. Go back. She's not in the forest. She's in the school."

Ashok's hands tightened. The voice continued, "No police. No press. Return to the school quietly. Or you'll never see the others."

Ashok froze, muttering back only fragmented responses: "Okay... alright... yes..."

The call ended.

"I need the van to stop," he said suddenly, his voice urgent. "We can't go to Laxmipuram. The caller said... my daughter is at the school. Right now."

Mrs. Renu turned sharply. "What?"

Ashok explained, breathless now. "They told me she's in the science lab. That she'll be handed over. But only if we go back. No forest. No police."

The driver pulled over near a roadside restaurant. Murmurs filled the van. Within moments, one of the officers dialled the IPS officer.

The Sudden Turnaround

Up ahead, the SUV had just taken a gentle curve when the IPS officer's phone rang. He picked it up, listening carefully.

"Sir," the officer said. "A parent received a call. He claims the girl is back at the school. He insists the voice sounded real."

The SUV slowed. The IPS officer looked back at Aryan.

"Turn around," he told the driver.

Aryan tilted his head. "Why are we going back?"

The officer hesitated. "They say one of the girls has been found."

Aryan didn't smile. He didn't celebrate. He only looked outside again; brows slightly furrowed.

Back at the restaurant stop, the convoy regrouped. The IPS officer took the call directly this time. Ashok explained again, his voice cracking. "Sir, he knew her name. He knew exactly where she'd be. And he said, if we keep looking in the forest, the others will vanish forever."

The IPS officer ended the call and quickly phoned the school.

"Check the science lab. Right now."

Shock at the School

Ten minutes later, the principal called back, voice trembling. "She's here. Unconscious. In the storage corner of the science lab. We've called an ambulance."

The entire convoy turned around. Every driver, every passenger—focused.

Ashok's hands trembled as he dialled again. The same voice answered. This time, calmer.

"You listened. Good. The other four are nearby. One in the football field. Two by the storeroom. No cops, or next time it'll be ten kids. Or more."

The call ended.

Back at the school, the gates were open. A small crowd had gathered already. An ambulance stood near the entrance, lights blinking.

Teachers ushered the police and parents in. Aryan walked quietly behind the others.

Inside the science lab, Asha was found lying curled in a corner. Her breathing was shallow but steady.

Ashok collapsed to his knees. Tears ran down his face. "Asha... Asha..."

Paramedics gently moved her onto a stretcher.

Uncovering the Others

Before they could speak further, Ashok's phone rang again.

"They're still waiting," the voice said. "No sirens. No uniforms. Find them quietly."

Two plainclothes officers, along with Mrs. Renu and the IPS officer, moved to the football field. At the far edge, hidden under an old football post, two more girls lay unconscious on the grass.

They were alive.

At the back of the campus, the old security storeroom was unlocked. The smell of stale chemicals lingered. A torch revealed the other two girls—near shelves of rusted paint tins and cleaning liquids. They were limp, but breathing.

All five had been returned.

Paramedics worked rapidly. Three ambulances now stood on standby.

A Silent Witness

Aryan stood still in the corridor, watching as girls were carried out one by one. Parents cried. Teachers sobbed. Some students peeked from windows.

Aryan didn't flinch.

His mother approached. "Aryan... they're all alive. They're okay."

He nodded. "For now."

At the Hospital

The hospital lobby buzzed with urgency. Doctors and nurses rushed between rooms. The IPS officer sat quietly at the edge of the waiting hall. The principal was beside him, pale and restless.

Then the hospital's landline rang.

A receptionist answered. After a pause, she approached the principal.

"There's a call for you."

The principal hesitated, then picked it up.

"You found them," the voice said. "Good. But don't celebrate yet. We're watching. Stop the investigation. No press. No names. Or next time—it won't be five."

The line disconnected.

She walked to the IPS officer and whispered the conversation.

He stood slowly. Walked to the centre of the room. And said, loud enough for all parents and teachers to hear:

"We're not dealing with one person. This is an organized threat."

The principal whispered, "Sir, if this becomes public... the school's reputation... the safety of others..."

The IPS officer opened his leather folder. Inside were marked reports and photos.

"In the past 32 years," he said, "nearly 10,000 girls have gone missing from this belt. Most never found. Most quietly filed away."

Gasps. One parent nearly collapsed.

Aryan looked around. His hand gripped his mother's.

The officer continued, "They chose this school because no one would suspect it. But this time—we got them back. And that means something. We're not stopping. We're going to find out who they are."

He turned to Aryan.

"And we're going to need you again."

Aryan didn't respond with words.

He only nodded.

Chapter 10: The Quiet Exit

Aftermath in the Hospital

The hospital's waiting area had grown still. The earlier chaos—sirens, shouting, frantic footsteps—had ebbed, replaced by low murmurs and the occasional rustle of medical charts. The children had been found. Panic had passed. But what lingered now was more unsettling: silence born not of relief, but of retreat.

Nurses moved softly across the marble floors, whispering updates. Doctors murmured at the end of the hallway, sharing reports in coded tones. Outside the examination rooms, parents clutched each other's hands or sat with vacant stares, their minds still replaying the unthinkable.

A Command to Withdraw

The IPS officer stood near the reception, quietly instructing his team. His expression remained composed but slightly resigned.

"Pull back," he said firmly. "The principal, the parents—even the students—they're unwilling to speak further. We won't press. We've done our part. Let's leave quietly."

His officers exchanged glances, some nodding with regret. They had come to act, to resolve something bigger than a single school incident. But now their uniforms felt heavy—not with medals, but with mistrust.

They had been told: stop asking questions. No interviews. No names in the press. The institution's reputation was paramount, and everyone had agreed—consciously or out of fear—that silence was safer.

A Glance Between Worlds

From across the room, Aryan stood near his parents. His gaze wandered—not curious, not alarmed. Just still. His body leaned slightly to one side as if he were leaning into a thought only, he could hear. His mother gently squeezed his hand, but Aryan didn't respond. He was somewhere else.

The IPS officer's eyes found him. Their stares met. For a moment, neither blinked.

A tired father. A thoughtful boy. A man who had seen enough battles to know when words were empty.

Then, Aryan's father leaned down. He whispered something to his son. The two slipped quietly into the corridor.

The officer noticed. He said nothing. No orders. No pursuit.

Waiting in the Night

Instead, he stepped outside.

The night air greeted him with a breeze. The scent of rain still lingered from earlier in the evening. A few vehicles idled nearby—marked police cars and a plain black SUV. Streetlamps flickered above like tired sentinels.

He opened the back door of the SUV and sat down, his cap still in hand. His eyes remained fixed on the hospital entrance. It was glass-panelled, bright, open—but felt impenetrable.

"Don't start the engine," he told his driver.

"Yes, sir."

And so, they waited.

An Hour of Stillness

Ten minutes. Then twenty. The officer said nothing. He simply leaned back in his seat; arms folded loosely across his chest. Occasionally, he glanced at his watch. Occasionally, he watched the front doors.

More nurses exited, chatting in soft voices. An elderly man was escorted out in a wheelchair. A delivery boy brought in a food packet for a ward nurse. But Aryan did not appear.

At the thirty-five-minute mark, one of the plainclothes officers came up to the window.

"Sir, should we return to base?"

The IPS officer waved him off.

"Give it time."

The officer retreated. The SUV remained idle.

At the forty-five-minute mark, the IPS officer took out his phone. He opened the messaging app. A message from the Chief Superintendent blinked on the screen: **"Update?"**

He typed: **"All five recovered. But full silence from the school. Investigative direction has collapsed."**

He stared at the blinking cursor.

Then he added: **"But there's something else. A boy. I'll explain later."**

He didn't press send.

Departure

At the fifty-five-minute mark, he glanced again toward the entrance. The glass doors reflected the ambulance lights. A nurse was sipping tea near the vending machine. Two ward boys chatted about the power fluctuations in the ICU.

Still no sign of Aryan.

At exactly one hour, the IPS officer straightened his spine, placed his cap back on his head, and said, "Let's go."

The driver started the vehicle. The convoy behind them blinked to life in sequence.

The SUVs, jeeps, and sedans turned one by one onto the darkened road, their headlights cutting lines through the mist. The tires hummed against the wet tar. Behind them, the hospital shrank into a block of light. The murmurs, the waiting families, the silent boy—left behind.

The IPS officer didn't look back.

But his mind stayed there.

The Boy Behind the Door

Back inside, the hospital corridor remained dim. At the end of the hallway, the examination rooms glowed under dull ceiling lamps. A faint antiseptic smell floated through the air.

Inside one of the rooms, Aryan sat on a small bench, flanked by his parents. A doctor stood in front of him with a clipboard.

"Does he remember anything else?" the doctor asked.

"No," Aryan's father answered. "He hasn't said a word since the return."

Aryan's mother placed her hand on her son's knee. "We're taking him home tomorrow. Far away from here."

The doctor nodded. "He's healthy. But... watch his sleep. And if he starts drawing again, let someone know."

Aryan's eyes didn't move. He wasn't sleeping. He wasn't blinking. He was just... there.

Outside the window, the streetlamps hummed.

The police were gone.

But something else had remained.

Chapter 11: The Silent Storm

A Still Night Shattered

The night air outside the hospital was crisp, unnaturally still after the retreat of the police vehicles. The parking area, lit by tall, flickering streetlights, looked deserted, a stage set for something waiting to unfold. Aryan, flanked by his father and mother, walked slowly toward their car. His small hand was held firmly in his father's—more a tether than comfort. Every step felt heavy.

Fifteen minutes had passed since the IPS officer and his team departed. Their absence left behind an eerie void. Footsteps echoed faintly on the asphalt. The silence was absolute.

Then, it shattered.

The whine of engines sliced through the quiet. A new convoy of police jeeps roared down the road, sirens off but lights spinning red and blue. Two ambulances trailed behind. Tires screeched as vehicles pulled into the hospital's emergency bay.

Before they had even come to a full stop, doors flew open and officers and medics jumped out. Stretchers rolled. Shouts broke through the air.

The Return in Blood

Aryan's father instinctively shielded his son. He watched in alarm as the doors of one ambulance flew open, revealing a stretcher soaked in blood. A man in uniform lay on it—groaning, hard pressed to his side. On the second stretcher, another body lay limp, still.

Aryan's father approached one of the arriving officers. "What happened?"

"Ambush," the officer panted. "Bypass road. The IPS officer's car... attacked. Two gunshot wounds—shoulder and bicep. He's lucky. The driver... he's critical. Took a bullet to the chest. Crashed into a truck."

Aryan stared, unmoving.

The police had only just pulled away. Now they returned, broken.

Urgency Within Walls

Inside the hospital, chaos unfolded with clinical urgency. The sterile scent of antiseptic mixed with sweat, blood, and adrenaline. Medical teams snapped into action; their faces locked in grim concentration.

The IPS officer was wheeled in, still conscious. Blood coated the left side of his uniform. His breathing was ragged, his hand gripping the edge of the stretcher. His eyes, though, remained focused. Defiant. He met Aryan's gaze for the briefest of moments as he passed, then closed his eyes as a nurse inserted a sedative.

The driver followed. He was pale. His breathing came in shallow gasps. Paramedics worked over him as they rushed past Aryan and his family. A nurse was already applying pressure to his chest wound. There was no time to spare.

Aryan's mother held his shoulders. The boy didn't resist. He sat quietly as doctors and officers stormed past.

Media Gathers, Truth Scatters

News spread quickly.

Within the hour, the hospital grounds transformed. Media vans pulled up. Reporters swarmed the entrance, shouting into cameras. Flashbulbs lit the night. The names of the injured were not yet released, but whispers had begun.

Inside, a press conference was hastily arranged.

A senior officer emerged with a statement. "The IPS officer is stable. He's in surgery. Prognosis is hopeful. The driver is in critical condition. We are monitoring him closely."

"What happened?" a reporter shouted.

"An ambush. Two suspects engaged. Before they could be apprehended, they took their own lives. The investigation continues."

Gasps rippled through the room.

"Forensics is working on ID. The attackers had no documentation. Facial reconstruction will take time. We expect preliminary reports within forty-eight hours."

No more questions. The officers returned inside.

A Familiar Stranger Arrives

Back in the waiting area, Aryan sat on a metal bench, feet dangling. His eyes were blank. His fingers traced slow circles on the steel surface beside him.

Across the corridor, his father stood by the vending machine, arms crossed. His mother remained seated, silently watching the emergency wing.

Then—

A shadow moved at the far end.

Shankar Kaka.

He appeared like a memory—not announced, not expected. Just present. He carried a faded cloth bag, his posture more hunched than before. He walked slowly, past the main entrance, toward the emergency wing.

"Stop right there," one officer said, stepping forward.

Kaka stopped. "I work in the IPS officer's home," he said, voice trembling. "I brought his medicines. And his file."

Two officers flanked him. One radioed in. Moments later, a familiar face appeared—an assistant from the IPS officer's team. He gave a curt nod.

"Let him in."

Kaka passed by Aryan. Their eyes met. Neither spoke.

Endless Waiting

Time ticked by.

Aryan sat unmoving. The hospital corridor began to thin out as morning neared. Parents of the rescued girls came and went. Some prayed. Some cried. Others just waited.

Aryan's family remained. The boy had not asked to leave. He hadn't spoken since they sat down.

A nurse offered them water. Aryan refused. His father took it, sipped, and placed the cup back down.

In a nearby room, the IPS officer's surgery concluded. The doctors emerged.

"He's stable," one of them said to the officer's assistant. "Rest is critical. No stress. No visitors for now."

The driver was still in surgery.

A sudden hush fell over the hallway.

An officer stepped out from the surgical wing and approached Aryan's father.

"He asked for your son," the officer said quietly. "Just once. In his sleep. He said Aryan's name."

The father looked at Aryan.

"I don't want to go," Aryan said, his voice faint.

The officer understood.

Dawn of Something Deeper

Hours passed. The crowd outside lessened. The media moved to another story. The parents began to trickle home.

But Aryan stayed.

As dawn broke, the temple bell rang.

And Aryan finally blinked.

Chapter 12: The Ice Rose Connection

Tension in the Halls

The hospital corridors were quieter now, but the silence was deceiving. Beneath it pulsed tension—tight, brittle, waiting to snap. Every footstep echoed like a dropped pin on marble. Nurses whispered in corners, carrying charts and adjusting IVs, their eyes betraying concern. Uniformed officers maintained their posts near doors and staircases. Outside, behind the glass walls, reporters paced restlessly like hounds straining against their leashes.

Aryan sat close to his father on the cool steel bench outside the ICU, his small frame leaning against his parent. His mother rubbed his back slowly, her eyes darting between the clock and the ICU doors. The long night had not yet loosened its grip on them.

A Request from Within

The double doors to the ICU creaked open. A doctor stepped out—mid-fifties, greying temples, thick glasses slightly askew. He looked exhausted, his coat wrinkled and streaked with evidence of a night that hadn't ended.

"Is there someone named Aryan here?" he asked the waiting families.

Aryan's father stood immediately, tension rising in his voice. "Yes. My son. Why?"

The doctor approached, speaking low. "The IPS officer... he keeps murmuring your son's name. He's weak but conscious. He refuses to calm down. Says he needs to see Aryan. It seems important."

There was a long pause.

Aryan's father looked down at his son. Then, sensing the urgency beyond words, he nodded and took Aryan's hand.

Inside the ICU

The air inside was thick—sterile but heavy. Monitors beeped. The soft rhythm of ventilators and IV drips echoed. Beds were partitioned with pale blue curtains. The smell of antiseptic clung to everything.

Aryan walked slowly, gripping his father's hand. When they reached the corner bed, the IPS officer was lying back, arm bandaged, oxygen tubes tucked under his nose. He looked fragile, his strength hollowed out.

But when Aryan stepped closer, the man's eyes opened wide with recognition.

"Aryan," he breathed.

Aryan stepped forward. "I am here, sir."

A Memory Shared

The officer smiled weakly. "Tell me... why did you ask for ice rose milk... with cherry on top?"

The room stilled.

"You know," he continued, voice hoarse, "it was my favourite. My daughter's too. Every summer, we waited for

Shankar Kaka to bring it. Even now... she still asks for it. And me... I never stopped loving it."

Nurses stopped what they were doing. Doctors glanced over. Something deep had surfaced.

Aryan turned toward the doorway where Shankar Kaka stood. "Kaka," he said gently, "can I have an ice rose milk... with cherry on top?"

Shankar Kaka stepped forward slowly, eyes moist. From his cloth bag, he pulled a small steel flask and a covered glass. The contents were poured carefully—chilled rose milk, creamy pink. A red cherry was gently dropped in.

He handed the glass to Aryan with shaking hands.

A Bridge Across Generations

The IPS officer chuckled, tears slipping from his eyes. "Just like old times, Kaka."

Aryan walked over. "You're a good officer, sir. I want to become like you."

The man's lips trembled. His eyes closed momentarily, as though holding onto the moment.

The doctor approached Aryan gently. "He needs rest. You've done more than enough."

Aryan nodded, stepping back. But the IPS officer wasn't done.

"Escort Aryan's family," he rasped. "With protection. Armed. He's in danger... too."

The senior officer outside acted instantly. Radio commands followed. Within minutes, two armed guards positioned themselves beside Aryan's parents.

They looked at each other—startled. Real fear now crept into their bones.

Under Guard

The ride home was unlike any they'd known. Their family car was flanked by two police jeeps, one ahead, one behind. Officers with rifles scanned every alley, every rooftop. Aryan leaned against his father, too tired to speak. His mother held his hand tightly.

The city was strangely still. No honking, no pedestrians. The morning sun seemed too harsh, filtered through a hazy sky.

When they reached their house, the officers jumped out first. The perimeter was scanned. Only when they gave the signal were Aryan and his parents allowed to step inside.

Two officers stayed back—one at the front gate, one at the rear.

Inside the Home

Curtains were drawn. Doors locked. The home was dimmed into a protective womb.

Aryan changed into fresh cotton clothes and quietly went to his room. His mother placed a hand on his back as he passed, but he said nothing.

In his room, the rose milk sat on the nightstand. The cherry still floated, its red stark against the pink.

He lay down. Sleep didn't come immediately—but it came.

In the Shadows

Outside, a man stood beyond the streetlights—just far enough not to be seen. He wore a dark cap and held a phone to his ear.

"They've returned. Two armed guards. The boy is safe... for now."

A pause.

Then he added, "We wait. But not for long."

He turned and disappeared into the alley as the sun broke fully over the city.

Chapter 13: The Welcome Bell

The Return to School

It was quite a sunny day. The sky looked clear, with just a few clouds scattered across the bright blue above Aryan's neighbourhood. The air was warm, still, and dry. Sunlight filtered through the trees that lined the compound wall of Aryan's house, casting scattered shadows on the cement ground. The gentle chirp of birds from above the boundary wall gave a peaceful rhythm to the morning.

Aryan stepped out from the house, wearing his school uniform — his shirt properly tucked in, a neatly tightened tie, polished shoes, and a school bag hanging from his shoulder. He looked fresh and a little more grown up than he did a month ago. Beside him walked his father, holding the bike keys, with quiet pride and concern in his eyes.

It had been nearly thirty days since Aryan had last gone to school — and a lot had changed in that time. What had started as a simple school excursion to Laxmipuram had turned into something unforgettable, unsettling, and mysterious. The aftermath of his drawing, the missing girls, and the police investigations had shaken many. Today, however, Aryan was ready to step back into school life — and he wanted his father to take him.

Normally, Aryan would go to school on his bicycle. It was just a short distance, a kilometre or so — a ride he always enjoyed. But the school had strictly instructed his parents not to allow him to travel alone anymore. They were either to send him by the school van or personally drop and pick him up. So, when Aryan said to his father softly, "Father, I want you to take me to school today," it came from the heart — and his father agreed instantly.

A Joyful Surprise

As they stepped out to the front gate, the school van — a familiar orange and white vehicle — pulled up in front of the house. Its engine let out a low rumble as it came to a halt. The driver, Ramesh's uncle, gave a small honk and looked out the window. But before either Aryan or his father could wave, the real surprise came from inside the van.

The entire van was filled with voices of excited students yelling, "Aryan! Aryan!"

One of the little kids inside pressed his face against the window glass and smiled wide. Another younger child shouted his name with joy. The chorus of his name filled the street for a few moments.

The school van driver shouted from his seat, "Don't make noise while the van is moving!" trying to control the excited children. Aryan's father smiled and gestured to Aryan, "They're happy to see you, son." Aryan gave a small wave, visibly overwhelmed by the attention.

The motorbike started, and Aryan sat behind his father. As the bike moved forward, Aryan, with a spark in his eyes, leaned forward and whispered,

"Father, overtake the van."

His father chuckled but picked up the speed. The bike slowly overtook the van, and as they passed by the windows, the students inside clapped and waved. Aryan smiled for the first time that morning — genuinely, shyly, and with gratitude.

Eyes on Aryan

At last, the bike stopped at the entrance of the school. The moment they arrived, a security person in uniform rushed forward. He greeted Aryan's father with a slight nod and looked toward Aryan.

"Please move quickly to your class, Aryan," he said politely. "The principal has instructed that you be escorted."

Aryan, now slightly nervous, looked back at his father. His father gave him an encouraging pat on the back. "Go on, champ. Everyone's waiting for you."

And with that, Aryan stepped into the school campus, walking beside the security guard. His bag bounced gently against his back. The moment he crossed the gate; all eyes were on him. Students standing in groups in the corridor turned to look. Some teachers near the staffroom paused and glanced at him with a mix of surprise and emotion.

It was as if an alien had walked in — or perhaps, a hero. Aryan felt the weight of those eyes, but kept walking, quietly.

Back Among Friends

From the corridor ahead, another boy came rushing toward him — Rohan. His best friend. His partner in everything. The moment Rohan saw Aryan, his face lit up and he jogged to meet him.

"Aryan!" he said, slowing down and matching steps with him. "You finally came!"

Aryan smiled, more comfortably now, and nodded. "Yes, I wanted to come today."

Together, they walked toward the classroom. Now, both of them were the centre of attention. Whispers filled the corridor. Other students smiled, nudged each other, pointed quietly. A few even followed behind to see what would happen.

As they reached the entrance of their classroom, Aryan stepped inside, and in that very moment —

the entire class stood up and started clapping

Chapter 14: The Second Sketch

A Standing Ovation

The sound of clapping filled the classroom, echoing off the old cement walls and wooden desks. The ceiling fans hummed quietly above, but all that could be heard was the cheerful applause from his classmates. It wasn't dramatic — it was genuine, and it stunned Aryan for a moment.

He stood just inside the doorway, looking at everyone with wide eyes. Even the teacher who was already in the class

— a soft-spoken middle-aged woman in a cotton sari — joined in, smiling warmly as she gently clapped along with the students.

Rohan, still beside him, turned with pride and started clapping too. "Come on," he whispered with a grin, "you have to enjoy this!"

Aryan was confused at first, unsure whether to smile, cry, or hide. But the warmth of the moment slowly melted his nervousness. He stepped forward, looking around as every desk turned toward him like sunflowers toward the sun.

As the applause faded, the teacher spoke gently, "Welcome back, Aryan. We missed you."

Aryan nodded slightly, unable to say much. The weight of 30 days away, of questions unanswered, of dreams drawn and real stories unfolding — it all seemed to pause in that moment.

Classroom Kindness

The class resumed. Aryan sat beside Rohan, and for the next couple of hours, different teachers came in. But what surprised Aryan was that each teacher who entered took a moment to acknowledge his return. They paused, smiled, some clapped again, and one even said with a slightly choked voice, "It's good to see you here."

Aryan felt strange. Not because he was being noticed — but because everyone was being so kind.

One teacher after another came — six in total — each leaving behind a moment of encouragement or warmth. Aryan, shy as he was, even clapped for himself once or twice when the class did. Everyone laughed.

By the time the final class of the day came — Art class — Aryan felt a little lighter. Rohan had kept him engaged the whole time, whispering jokes, telling stories, nudging him whenever a teacher looked away. The two of them were inseparable, and today, it was as if nothing had happened. Almost.

Best Friends Forever

As they walked to the art room, Rohan turned to the class and loudly declared, "Aryan is my best friend. Right, Aryan?"

Aryan looked at him, smiled without hesitation, and replied softly, "Yes. You are my one very best friend."

The hallway echoed with a few "Awes" and cheerful teasing. But Rohan looked like he had just won a trophy. He walked into the art room with his head held high.

Imagination Over Instruction

Ravi — a calm, enthusiastic young teacher with greying hair, sharp spectacles, and paint on his fingers — stood near the big blackboard, waiting for them. His apron was already smudged with colour, and a large glass jar full of sketch pens, pencils, and crayons sat beside him.

As the students filed in, he looked over his glasses and said, "Today, we are not going to draw from a textbook. You'll draw what's in your mind. Whatever you've seen, dreamt, felt — put it on paper. Don't copy. Imagine."

The students began to settle down, murmuring excitedly about what to draw. But most of them were also looking toward Aryan, curious. What would he draw this time?

The art sir, noting the attention on Aryan, quietly walked up to him and said, "You sit in the far corner, Aryan. That way, no one disturbs you. Take your time."

Return of the Vision

Aryan obeyed silently, picking a corner desk — far from the centre of the room — and took out a blank sheet of paper. The sounds of pencils scratching, erasers squeaking, and chairs shifting filled the room. The sunlight streamed in through the grilled windows, catching little particles of dust in the air, turning the room golden.

For a moment, everything went still for Aryan. He picked up the pencil and closed his eyes — and once again, that vision returned. The same image. The bus. The bridge. The borewell. The girl.

Chapter 15: The Sketch Without Shadows

A New Beginning

With pencil in hand, Aryan slowly began sketching.

At first, just faint outlines.

He drew the back seat of a school bus, carefully shaping the curve of the window. Then, he added a small figure — a boy — kneeling on the seat, his knees pressed into the cushion, arms resting on the window frame. The boy's head was tilted slightly, as if peering into the distance.

Next, Aryan drew the outside view: Far in the distance, he placed a borewell handpump — old, metallic, familiar. Beside the pump stood a girl, her figure facing the bus, one hand extended, one finger pointing directly toward the forest beyond.

But this time — this time, there were no five girls drawn inside the forest.

Just trees. Just open space. Just the direction she pointed.

His strokes were slow but confident. He didn't look around. He didn't hesitate. He just drew. Around him, the class began finishing up. Bags zipped, chairs scraped, the chatter began again. But Aryan remained focused.

Ravi, walking between rows, nodded at students' sketches. When he reached Aryan's corner, he stopped.

He saw the sketch.

His eyes narrowed. He said nothing. And then the bell rang.

Eyes on the Page

Students rose, grabbing bags. A few drifted to Aryan's desk.

Someone whispered, "Is that the same one?" Another said, "No, the girls aren't there this time." Another muttered, "But the rest is exactly the same..."

Ravi raised his hand. "Everyone, out now. Aryan will stay a little longer. His parents will pick him up. The social teacher will escort him to the gate."

Students left slowly. Rohan was last, flashing Aryan a thumb-up. "It's amazing," he mouthed.

Ravi leaned closer. "Finish this drawing at home tonight, Aryan. Bring it to me tomorrow. You've captured something..." He paused. "...something important."

Aryan nodded.

The Reaction

Minutes later, the social teacher arrived. She wore a simple blue saree and spectacles, calm and thoughtful.

"Good evening, Aryan."

"Good evening, teacher," he replied.

She approached. "What are you drawing today?"

Aryan handed her the paper.

She took it and glanced at the sketch.

Her smile vanished.

Her eyes scanned the boy, the bus, the borewell, the pointing girl, and the forest.

A visible shiver passed through her.

Without a word, she turned and exited the art room.

In the corridor, she pulled out her phone and called the principal.

"Sir… we need to talk. I've seen another drawing. I think it's… important."

The principal's voice was calm. "Bring it to the office. Tell Aryan to stay in the art room. I'll call his parents."

She hung up.

Then dialled again — not to the principal.

To the police.

"We may have a development," she said. "Please come immediately. Quietly. This may involve the same student."

Chapter 16: The Questioning

Quiet in the Corner

Back in the art room, Aryan remained seated in the corner, exactly where he had been told. His sketchbook lay in front of him, the drawing partially complete. He began sketching another image — just doodles, really. A small tree. The sun. A sloping path. A quiet escape from the emotions brewing around him.

The room had grown quiet. The other chairs stood empty. Only the soft creaking of the fan and the scratching of his pencil on paper could be heard.

A few feet away, near the doorway, stood the school maid — an elderly woman in her fifties with a warm face, neatly tied back hair, and a dupatta covering her head. She had been assigned to stay with Aryan until his parents arrived. Occasionally, she glanced at him with the affection of a grandmother, her eyes full of unspoken concern.

An Arrival in Silence

Outside, the atmosphere shifted.

The sound of a siren — faint at first — grew louder. It wasn't panicked or dramatic, but deliberate and controlled. It came from the back of the school, near the side entrance. Two police vehicles turned slowly into the school compound, bypassing the main gate to avoid drawing attention.

The principal, standing at the entrance of his office, saw them arrive and quickly gestured to park out of view. A few parents waiting outside turned, curious, but were told politely by the security to stay calm — "Routine check, nothing serious."

Inside the office, the social teacher entered, holding Aryan's drawing in her hands. She laid it gently on the principal's table.

The principal adjusted his glasses and looked at it. His expression froze.

A minute later, Aryan's parents arrived — having been called only ten minutes earlier. Aryan's mother looked worried. His father looked serious.

They walked in and saw the drawing lying flat on the table.

"Did he draw this here?" the father asked.

The social teacher nodded. "Just now. In art class."

Aryan's mother took a step forward and whispered, "There's no one in the forest…"

"Yes," said the principal. "This time, no girls. Just the same borewell, the same bridge, the same pointing girl."

Inside the Drawing

The police entered silently. One officer leaned toward the desk and studied the paper.

"Does he say who the girl is?" the officer asked.

"No," said the social teacher. "But… he always draws her."

The principal turned to Aryan's parents; his voice low but steady. "I know this is difficult. But we need to ask him about this drawing. We must understand what he's seeing — or remembering."

Aryan's father sighed. "We've already told you everything. He doesn't speak of the trip. He only mentioned once that he wants to go back to Laxmipuram. That's all."

The police nodded. "We will not scare the boy. But we need to speak to him."

The principal nodded in agreement. "Let's do it gently."

The Conversation

Inside the art room, the maid turned as the principal and Aryan's parents entered together. Behind them came two policemen, dressed in plain clothes.

Aryan looked up, surprised.

His mother smiled softly. "Son, how are you feeling?"

"I'm fine," he said. "I was just finishing my drawing."

His father sat beside him and put a hand on his back. "Some people want to ask you a few questions. Just answer honestly, okay?"

Aryan nodded, unsure.

One of the officers knelt down, holding the drawing. "Aryan, can I ask you something? Why did you draw this girl again?"

Aryan looked at the paper and said, "She's always there. Every time I close my eyes on the bus… I see her."

The officer's voice was gentle. "And she's pointing?"

"Yes. Toward the forest."

"Did you see her during the trip?"

"No," Aryan shook his head. "Only… in my mind."

"Why didn't you draw the five girls like last time?"

Aryan looked confused. "What five girls? I didn't draw anyone else."

Everyone in the room exchanged glances.

"You did, son," his mother said carefully. "Last time, there were five girls in the forest."

Aryan blinked. "But… I never drew them. Only the girl near the borewell."

The officer sat back slowly. "He doesn't know."

The principal looked tense. "So, he's not imagining it. The earlier drawing must have come from something deeper..."

A Hidden Motive

Another officer stepped outside to make a call.

The lead officer stood. "We'll have to go back. We must look at the spot again. But with care this time."

He paused and glanced at the principal.

"There's something else," he said quietly. "We weren't called here because of the drawing."

The principal looked confused. "But... the teacher contacted you."

The officer shook his head. "We were already on our way here. We had reason to believe something else was unfolding inside this school today. The drawing only confirms we're on the right path."

The principal frowned. "Then why didn't you come through the main gate?"

The officer's voice was firm now. "Because if someone inside the school is watching — we didn't want them to know we were already here."

Chapter 17: The Shadow Beside the

Fountain

A Quiet Exit

As the officers stepped aside to confer with the principal, Aryan quietly packed away his pencil and placed the unfinished drawing inside his sketchbook. The school maid returned with a bottle of water and a small packet of biscuits, placing them gently on his desk. He nodded politely.

The social teacher returned, holding her phone in one hand. "Aryan," she said kindly, "your parents are waiting at the main gate. I'll walk you there."

Aryan stood, picked up his bag, and followed her. The school maid walked a few paces behind, keeping an eye on him as if he were her own grandson. The corridors were quiet now, the low echo of their footsteps the only sound between the walls.

Farewells in the Hallway

As they approached the main block, the art sir passed them in the hallway.

"Aryan," he said warmly, "bring that drawing tomorrow — I want to see it finished."

Aryan smiled faintly and nodded. "Yes, sir."

The walk from the classroom block to the front gate felt long, lined with golden sunlight and long shadows. Aryan looked left and right, seeing familiar trees, the empty basketball court, and the flagpole. Everything looked normal — but felt different.

A Glimpse Beyond

At the gate, his father waited beside the bike. The moment he saw Aryan; he stepped forward and gently held his hand.

"Let's go, Aryan."

Aryan nodded, slipping his bag over his shoulder.

But just before getting onto the bike, he turned around one last time. He looked at the old fountain in the school courtyard — dry for years, shaped like a borewell.

And for a fraction of a second… he thought he saw the same girl standing beside it, arm outstretched, finger still pointing into something unseen.

But when he blinked, she was gone.

He climbed onto the bike behind his father. The sun was setting behind the school gates. The truth was still waiting.

And whatever she was pointing at… would have to wait for another day.

Chapter 18: What the Shadows Hid

A Return Unseen

The school gate shimmered under the late morning sun as Aryan sat on the bike. The engine hadn't started yet. His mind was still wandering in fragments of memory — the drawing, the whisper of the forest, the fountain and the girl, the silence that always followed when people saw what he drew. Behind him, the school campus stood still, its corridors emptying after the bell, the voices fading behind slowly shutting windows.

Just as Aryan's father kicked the rod to start the bike, a car rolled up silently to the gate.

There was no siren. No honk. But something about its presence stirred every adult around.

It was a white government vehicle — dust clinging lightly to its wheels, but polished, official, unmistakably familiar. As the car door opened, a short man — around 5 feet 6 inches tall, aged in his 50s — stepped out slowly.

Gasps were barely audible, but faces turned.

It was the IPS officer.

The same officer who had been shot — twice — just a month ago. The officer who had survived what many thought was an execution attempt. His return today, unannounced, without uniform, was not just a visit — it was a message.

An Unexpected Exchange

He wore plain clothes — a soft brown coat over a cream shirt, sleeves rolled neatly at the forearms, and dark sunglasses that barely hid the deep rings beneath his eyes. A scar peeked out beneath the collarbone — a reminder of the bullet wound. Yet, his posture was unshaken.

As he stepped toward Aryan's father, the two greeted each other wordlessly with a firm nod.

Just then, Aryan reached them.

"Sir… how are you?" Aryan asked, looking up at the officer.

The IPS officer turned, looked down at the boy, and a small smile escaped his lips.

"I'm doing well, Aryan," he said, his voice hoarse but composed. "What about you?"

"I'm good, sir," Aryan replied with a small smile.

Then, his tone lightened. "How is Shankar Kaka? And where is my drink?"

The IPS officer chuckled — a rare, warm sound from a man burdened with far too many secrets.

He turned to his assistant and said, "Bring him his bottle."

The assistant, who had just stepped out from the car, opened a cooler box and handed Aryan a chilled glass bottle filled with rose-flavoured milk, complete with a single cherry floating at the top.

Aryan received it with the delight of a child returning to a favourite moment. He unscrewed the cap and began drinking slowly, savouring it.

The Revelation in the Sketch

By then, the principal had arrived from the school building, holding a file in his hands, followed by another police officer. The drawing that Aryan had completed earlier — the one submitted through the social teacher — was inside the file.

The principal handed the file over to the IPS officer. Aryan's father and the officer opened it together, flipping through the thin sheets until they reached the one Aryan had drawn.

It was quiet again.

The same sketch: the boy in the bus, the girl at the borewell, her finger pointing.

But this time, the shaded region that earlier seemed abstract now had form.

Aryan, without lowering the bottle from his lips, spoke through sips.

"That drawing... it's incomplete," he said.

The IPS officer looked at him. "What do you mean?"

Aryan paused. Then calmly said, "In the dark part... the shadow... five women are being dragged into the forest."

A stunned silence fell on the group. Even the assistant holding the empty bottle stared at Aryan. The principal looked pale.

Aryan's father broke the silence, almost whispering: "Who... who are the women, Aryan?"

"I don't know," Aryan replied, unbothered. "But they were dragged. I saw it clearly."

A Second Glass, A Deeper Clue

The IPS officer did not react outwardly. Instead, he reached into the cooler once again, pulled out another chilled bottle, and offered it to Aryan.

"Would you like one more?" he asked.

Aryan nodded.

As he began drinking the second bottle, the IPS officer leaned forward. "Did you draw anything else? Recently?"

Aryan's eyes widened slightly as he nodded again. "Yes. After the social teacher left with the unfinished one... I drew one more."

"Can I see it?"

Aryan looked up at him.

"You don't need to," he said. "You can see it... in the maps."

Chapter 19: The Car in the Water

The Map in His Mind

For a moment, the statement seemed to hang in the air untouched — strange, still, and strangely heavy.

"You can see it... in the maps."

The IPS officer looked at Aryan with interest now.

"You said you drew one more... after the social teacher left?"

Aryan nodded, licking a bit of rose milk from his upper lip. "Yes, sir. I started another drawing when I was waiting. It's at home."

The officer's tone was calm. "Can I see it?"

Aryan opened his sketchbook and turned to the back page. He handed it carefully to the officer.

A Drowned Clue

It was another drawing — but not as clean or complete as the previous ones. A rough sketch of a river, dark shaded water... and something vague submerged below the surface.

The outline of a white car, partly underwater, was visible — but the rest of the image was incomplete. The lines were smudged, uncertain, almost hidden in the scribbled shadows.

The IPS officer squinted. "This... is a car?"

"Yes," Aryan said. "Submerged. In the river."

"But where exactly is it?" the officer asked. "This doesn't say where it is."

"I don't know how to draw places," Aryan said. "I just see what I see."

Searching for the Match

The IPS nodded slightly, turned to his assistant.

"Bring me the file set. Now."

The assistant returned moments later with a large black file case. The IPS placed it on the hood of the car and flipped it open. Inside were aerial photos, old missing reports, maps, and various photographs of known vehicles.

He began showing Aryan photo after photo.

"Is it this?" "No."

"This one?" "No, sir."

One after another — modern sedans, black SUVs, small hatchbacks — all were rejected.

Then came a slightly faded photograph of an old white Ambassador car, with two thick red and white diagonal stripes painted across its roof. It looked old, like something from another era, partly rusted but still intact.

Aryan leaned in; eyes fixed.

"This," he said. "It resembles this one."

The Missing Colour

The IPS raised an eyebrow. "But your drawing doesn't show any red on the roof."

Aryan replied plainly, "I didn't have a red pencil. I used black instead."

The officer paused, processing the honesty of the answer. He nodded slowly and tucked the photograph back inside.

Chapter 20: The Call That Changed Everything

Signals in Silence

Just then — the IPS officer's phone rang. As he held the
phone to his ear, his posture shifted.
He stood straighter. His hand, which had been resting
casually on the roof of the vehicle, clenched slightly. His
eyes locked on the ground as he listened in silence, his
face unreadable.

"Understood," he said into the receiver.
A pause.
"Yes, sir. We'll move. No official alert."
Another pause.
"No media, no memo. It's on me."

He ended the call.

Around him — Aryan's father, the principal, and two
junior officers — waited, expecting explanation. But the
IPS officer said nothing.

Orders in Motion

Without a word, he turned toward his assistant and
gestured subtly. The assistant pulled out a secondary
device — a walkie-talkie — and stepped aside to issue a
coded transmission.

The IPS officer then walked away from the group, far
enough to not be heard, and made a second, private phone
call.

His voice was sharp and focused.

"Mobilize a team. No sirens. Unmarked vehicles. Laxmipuram perimeter. Focus on river and old temple routes. Set up within the hour."

He ended the call without elaboration, then returned to the group, still keeping his intentions unspoken.

Turning to two plainclothes officers now stepping out of a support vehicle, he said:

"Take your bikes. Visit five households. Quietly. We're looking for connections — not suspects. Civil dress only. No uniforms."

The officers nodded, mounted their bikes, and departed.

Lockdown in Disguise

Next, the IPS officer approached the school principal, who was still standing at the gate with barely concealed unease.

"I want the school closed starting tomorrow. Two days. Announce it immediately."

The principal blinked, shocked.

"Sir... close the school? But—on what basis?"

"No explanations. No press notes. Just instructions," the IPS said flatly. "You'll get a confirmation call in two minutes."

Before the principal could protest further, his phone rang.

He stepped aside and answered.

"Yes, Chairman sir?"

The voice on the other end was composed but firm. "Close the school for the next two working days. State 'campus maintenance and interior rework.' Since it runs into the weekend, say classes resume after four days."

The principal stammered, "Yes, sir... I understand..."

"One more thing," the chairman added. "All teachers and staff must report. They'll be briefed. No one is exempt."

The call ended.

Still holding the phone, the principal turned toward the IPS and simply nodded, understanding that something larger than a campus repair was underway.

The Final Message

The IPS officer walked back to Aryan and his father.

A moment of silence passed between them. Aryan was finishing the last sips of his second rose milk bottle. His father stood beside him, still unsure what just happened or what was coming next.

As the officer turned to leave, Aryan casually looked up, like a child sharing a forgotten detail.

"You can see it," he said.

The IPS paused mid-step.

"In the maps," Aryan added, referring to the submerged car.

Everyone froze.

The IPS turned back, slow and deliberate.

"What did you say?"

Aryan pointed at his sketchbook. "The car. I don't know where it is on the ground. But I saw it. In the satellite maps. When I was zooming in the other day… it's there."

The IPS studied the boy for a long second. Then, unexpectedly gentle, he placed a hand on Aryan's shoulder.

Turning to Aryan's father, he said quietly:
"Take care of him. I'll be coming back."

Without another word, he returned to his vehicle.

No lights. No sirens.
The white government car pulled away from the school gate and disappeared into the shimmering heat.

Chapter 21: The Message Spread Silently

Stillness After the Visit

As the IPS officer's vehicle rolled away from the school gate and vanished into the blur of the afternoon heat, an uneasy stillness settled over the campus — the kind that arrives not with sound, but with the absence of it. It was the kind of silence that follows after something weighty has been said, but no one is ready to repeat it aloud.

Aryan stood beside the gate, gently licking the last trace of rose milk from the rim of the chilled bottle. His father took it from him, walked to a corner, and dropped it into a bin. The hollow thud it made was the only sound on the otherwise still campus.

Neither of them spoke.

The school gate, which had been bustling just minutes ago, now felt oddly deserted. Long shadows stretched across the pavement. Parents clustered in twos and threes, speaking in hushed tones, throwing curious glances at Aryan from a distance. A few younger students pointed and asked questions their parents didn't want to answer.

Near the office entrance, the principal stood with his phone still clutched in his hand. For a long time, he didn't move — until at last he turned, stepped inside his cabin, and softly closed the door behind him.

Orders had been given. Now came the execution.

Quiet Calls and Quiet Panic

Within ten minutes, the heads of departments began receiving short, cryptic instructions through calls and WhatsApp messages:

? *"School closed for four days. Reason: urgent renovation. Staff to report daily. Notify all students and parents."*

There were no detailed memos, no explanations, no warning from the morning assembly. The simplicity of the message made it more suspicious.

Inside the teachers' lounge, phones buzzed with notifications. Teachers began exchanging glances. The murmurs started instantly.

"Renovation? But we just had work done last term."

"They're calling everyone — even the bus drivers."

"This isn't about plumbing. Something's wrong."

One teacher looked around and muttered under her breath, "It's Aryan again, isn't it?"

No one replied. But no one denied it either.

Theories and Whispers

In staffrooms and empty corridors, theories began to spread like wildfire. Some rooted in fact. Some spiralling into absurdity.

"Wasn't there another drawing?"
"He sees something others can't..."
"There was a police vehicle today... what did they find?"

The younger teachers mostly stayed quiet. The senior staff tried to calm nerves. But the janitorial staff had already started talking — not just to each other, but outside the gates, to parents, to neighbours.

The story had already taken root — just not the official version.

Homes Flooded with Questions

Across the town, the news reached homes like a sudden wave. Parents received SMS alerts and voice calls from the school:

"Dear Parent, due to scheduled campus renovation, the school will remain closed for the next four days. Classes will resume after the weekend. All staff will remain on duty."

The responses were swift.

"Renovation? At this time of year?"
"But why are teachers going if students aren't?"
"Didn't something happen on that forest trip?"

WhatsApp groups exploded with speculation. Screenshots of Aryan's name. Snippets of old news clips. A blurred photo of the IPS officer arriving at the school gate. Everything was suddenly relevant. Everything felt connected.

At the Edge of the Gate

Back at the gate, Aryan and his father remained standing. There was no urgency to leave. Just a weight in the air they didn't know how to name.

Parents passed by with hesitant glances. Some smiled politely. Some said nothing. Some just stared, pretending not to.

Rohan came running up — backpack bouncing, breath short — and handed Aryan a small folded packet. "Cream biscuits," he said, whispering. "For the next four days. You'll draw something new, right?"

Aryan nodded. "I will."

Rohan hesitated, then added, "Tell me when you're ready. I'll be waiting."

Aryan smiled and replied softly, "I know."

Rohan waved and ran back to his mother, who gave a silent nod to Aryan's father before guiding her son away.

Inside the Staffroom

Elsewhere in the school, the principal stood alone inside the main staffroom, writing a notice on the whiteboard in red marker:

? **Mandatory Staff Assembly – 9:00 AM Tomorrow**
? **Venue: Main Conference Hall**
? *Attendance required for all departments, all staff, all designations.*

Below that was a handwritten list of every group:

- Teaching staff
- Transport team
- Peons
- Security guards
- Gardeners
- Janitors
- Maintenance crew

Everyone. No exceptions.

He stared at the board for a long moment.

This wasn't about maintenance. This wasn't about plumbing or ceiling repair. This wasn't even about the drawings anymore.

This was about a message — one that wasn't written down, but had already begun to travel. Like a ripple in still water.

A message that had reached the forest.
A message that had risen from the lake.
A message that had spread... silently.

Chapter 22: The Last Look Back

The Road After the Storm

The road outside the school stretched long and quiet under the afternoon light. Dust danced lazily along the edges, caught in small spirals by the breeze. The crowd had thinned. School bags had been slung onto shoulders. Children had gone home. And yet, Aryan and his father remained near the gate, standing still as if time around them had paused.

Some parents passed with brief nods or faint smiles. Others, unsure of what to say, simply avoided eye contact. They all knew something unusual had taken place — but no one was sure what it truly meant.

Across the yard, the school principal lingered a moment longer, watching the last IPS vehicle roll past the outer gate and disappear beyond the curve of the road. His hands were clasped behind his back, his expression unreadable.

Questions With No Answers

Back in the school corridors, the atmosphere remained tense. Teachers moved from room to room, packing up, collecting files, and sharing brief glances of confusion and concern. There was no final bell, no formal announcement — only silent decisions passed through whispered conversations.

"Four days?"
"Renovation, they say."
"Why call even the bus drivers and guards then?"

In the quietness, logic lost its footing. Everyone felt it. This wasn't just about paint or pipes. This was about something they weren't allowed to speak of — at least not yet.

Meanwhile, outside, Aryan and his father began walking slowly toward their parked bike. Aryan kept glancing down the road, toward the horizon, as if searching for something. Or someone.

They passed two school security guards speaking in hushed voices near the compound wall.

"I don't think this is just about renovation," one muttered.

Aryan didn't pause. He was listening — but only to the wind and the memory of a man who had left with a promise.

A Sudden Return

Just as Aryan swung his leg over the bike's side and prepared to ride pillion, a sound behind them made him stop.

The last police vehicle that had remained near the campus entrance began to move. Inside, the assistant of the IPS officer was speaking into a device, his tone careful, coded. The vehicle rolled forward.

But it wasn't alone.

Farther down the road, just beyond the final turn before the highway, the original IPS officer's vehicle — the one they had seen vanish earlier — returned.

It moved slowly, quietly.

It didn't pull up to the school. Instead, it stopped under the shade of a neem tree beside the edge of the boundary wall, just before the bend that disappeared into the distance.

And then, the door opened.

A Promise Before Departure

The IPS officer stepped out.

Alone. No escorts. No rush.

He walked a few steady steps back in the direction of Aryan and his father.

The two had paused now, seated on the bike but unmoving. The engine was running. But neither spoke.

The officer approached calmly, his coat slightly rustling in the wind. His face was calm — not serious, not soft — but somewhere in between.

He looked at Aryan's father, then at the boy.

Then, in a voice low enough for only them to hear, he said:

"Take care of your child."
"I will be coming back soon."

It wasn't a threat. It wasn't a request. It was a promise —
quiet, deliberate, and weighty.

Aryan looked up into the officer's face, his own expression
as calm as ever. His eyes didn't ask questions.

The IPS officer offered a slight nod — one final glance —
and turned.

He climbed back into the vehicle.

The door shut with a soft click. The car pulled away, this
time without hesitation. No pause. No rearview glance.

It vanished into the road's horizon.

The Silence Still Watching

Aryan and his father didn't speak for several seconds.
Then, without needing to say anything, Aryan placed his
hands lightly around his father's waist.

The bike moved forward.

The road behind them was empty once more. The school
gate closed slowly. The sun began to dip lower in the sky,
casting longer shadows across the yard and playground.

The mystery hadn't ended.

It had only gone quiet.

For now.

Somewhere beyond the roads, beyond the school, deeper
in the forest —
the girl still stood by the borewell.
Still pointing.
Still waiting.

Chapter 23: The Vanishing Mothers

They Dropped Their Daughters and Disappeared

The Day Aryan Returned — And So Did the Missing Girls

The morning began like any other school day. A gentle
orange hue lit the pavement in front of the school as the
sun crept up, soft and golden, filtered through the Gul
mohar and neem trees. The compound slowly began to
buzz with activity — school buses rolled in, bicycles
screeched to halts, and parents in cars and scooters
started to arrive, dropping off their children.

That very morning marked Aryan's first full day back at
school. The atmosphere had been curious and cautious
around him — teachers had exchanged glances, students
whispered, and even the principal had kept a discreet
watch. But amid this return to normalcy, something else
went unnoticed by most.

The five girls who had earlier gone missing — and were found under bizarre circumstances — had also returned to school the same day. They had arrived quietly with their mothers, slipping into the familiar routine of school life. There were no announcements. No questions. Just the illusion of calm.

Among the parents that morning were those five mothers — each of them returning to the school for the first time since the incident. After those tense, terrifying days when their daughters had disappeared and were found again, they had not let them out of sight.

Today marked the first day back to normal life — or at least, the appearance of it.

They arrived almost simultaneously, each in separate vehicles. One drove a grey sedan, another in a black SUV. The others came in a white hatchback, a maroon van, and an older beige Ambassador. The mothers parked carefully under the shade trees in the school parking lot. Their movements were measured, their faces serious — not hurried like most parents on a school morning, but careful and observant.

Each mother accompanied her daughter to the school gate, walking slowly, their eyes sweeping left and right, watching everything around. They greeted no one, didn't linger to chat with other parents, and only nodded briefly at the security staff as they entered the front path.

As their daughters crossed through the gates and disappeared into the building with the rest of the students, the mothers waited. None of them left immediately. One leaned against her car. Another made a call. A third stood near a tree, looking quietly toward the school building.

They had all spoken to their family members just moments before, saying nearly the same thing:

"We just dropped them off. We'll be home in two hours."

But none of them would return.

And none of them would answer their phones again.

Five Phones. One Tower. Zero Answers.

By noon, husbands, brothers, and parents of the five women began growing concerned. Calls were going unanswered. Texts remained unread. All five phones, one after the other, stopped ringing and switched off entirely. The last call received from each mother had been just outside the school gate.

Worried, each family — separately but almost simultaneously — contacted the police. Within hours, five reports had been registered. Five women. Missing. Last seen near the school. Last known calls traced to the same nearby mobile tower that covered the school premises.

The school management was unaware of any of this. No teacher, staff member, or official had noticed anything strange. From their perspective, the girls had come to class, and the morning was proceeding normally.

But at the local police control room, the five missing persons reports triggered a quiet escalation. When the police realized that all five phone signals dropped from the same location within the same window of time — and that the five women were the mothers of the same girls who had earlier vanished — the case changed instantly.

The details were relayed directly to the IPS officer.

He had barely finished reviewing a report on another case when the message arrived. He paused mid-sentence, his hand resting on a file, and read it twice.

Five missing again. But this time — the mothers.

Their phones had gone dark in the same radius. Near the school.

The IPS officer's face grew still.

He reached for his phone and placed a quick call.

"Send two of our best to the school now," he said. "Plain clothes. Keep eyes on the boy — Aryan. I'll follow."

Moments later, one of the two officers reached the school just as Aryan was showing his newest drawing to the art sir and social teacher. It was that moment — a glance at the sketch — that prompted the officer to step away and make a call back to the IPS.

"Sir," he said over the line, "you need to see this for yourself."

The IPS said nothing more. But ten minutes later, he was in the backseat of his unmarked vehicle, already en route, scanning a printed satellite map of the area surrounding the school.

He said nothing during the drive.

But in his mind, the investigation had already begun.

Chapter 24: The Envelope

An Invitation No One Expected

The Discovery

The moment the IPS officer received confirmation that the five mothers were officially missing, his instructions were swift and surgical.

"Mobilize five teams," he told his deputy. "Search each house. Full sweep. Quiet and thorough. I want everything documented."

Within the hour, unmarked police vehicles rolled into five separate residential areas across the city. The teams moved professionally; their presence kept discreet from curious neighbours. Inside each home, they moved carefully through every room, looking for any detail — a clue, a mark, a sign of forced entry, a misplaced object — anything that could explain why five women vanished on the same morning, from the same place, with no trace.

At first, the searches revealed nothing unusual. Kitchen items left untouched. Shoes still near the door. Purses left behind. It looked as if each woman had intended to return within minutes.

But then, in one home — and soon after in all five — something unusual was found.

It was a **maroon-coloured envelope**, thick and glossy, resting quietly on a table in the hallway. It wasn't hidden — just waiting to be noticed. The envelope was bordered in elegant **gold trim**, and printed neatly at the top in gold letters was the name of the woman it belonged to.

Inside the envelope, they found a single sheet of high-quality invitation paper — heavy, textured, and glowing faintly under the ceiling lights. It was an **invitation to a celebrity fashion show**, being held that very day at one of the most luxurious hotels in the city.

The same envelope was discovered — identical in design, paper, and content — in all five houses.

The news was relayed immediately to the IPS officer.

He didn't say anything for a moment after hearing it. Then, simply, "We're going to the hotel."

The Hotel That Held No Answers

By late afternoon, two police SUVs arrived at the hotel, escorted by a security liaison. The building stood tall against the orange sky — gleaming glass panels reflecting the fading sun, a long red carpet still laid out in front, now mostly empty except for a few staff cleaning up.

Inside the main lobby, the receptionist and hotel manager were already waiting, briefed by a junior officer. The IPS officer walked in without hesitation.

"We're here about five women," he said. "We need access to parking records, security footage, and every floor of this building."

The manager complied. The fashion show, he explained, had just concluded an hour ago. It had been a closed event. High-profile. Invites only. No press allowed.

The CCTV room was on the basement level. There, in a narrow room lined with monitors and buzzing hardware, the footage began to play.

The security recordings showed all five vehicles — the grey sedan, black SUV, white hatchback, maroon van, and an electric vehicle — pulling into the underground parking lot one after another that morning. All between 10:25 and 10:40 AM.

But something was wrong.

None of the recordings showed the women exiting their vehicles.

There were no visuals of them entering the lobby, walking into the fashion hall, or anywhere on the main floors of the hotel.

It was as if the cars had arrived... and then vanished into thin air.

The Vehicles Remained, But the People Were Gone

The officers rushed down to the parking levels.

There they were — all five cars. Still in place. But randomly positioned, as if parked hurriedly or without coordination. One was slightly skewed in the corner. Another had its headlights still faintly blinking, drained of battery.

The IPS officer paced slowly through the rows of parked vehicles, silent. He ran his fingers along the hood of one car. Still faintly warm.

Back in the control room, the footage inside the fashion show hall was reviewed.

Nothing.

The cameras captured the audience, the models, the organizers — but not a single frame showed any of the five women.

None of the staff remembered seeing them. No check-ins matched their names. No witnesses.

It didn't make sense.

That's when the IPS officer stepped back and reached for his phone.

He remembered Aryan's words.

"Five women... dragged into the forest."

He pulled up Aryan's sketch on his phone. The borewell. The finger pointing. The shadow line along the tree edge.

The officer called the **search team stationed near Laxmipuram**.

"Start again," he said sharply. "It's getting dark — take the torches. Begin from the borewell. Move toward the forest line."

There was no room for error now.

The forest had to be searched — not just for what it hid, but for what it might try to keep.

Chapter 25: The Warning

A brutal message delivered in blood. The enemy steps into

the light.

The Forest Mission Begins

The forest search had just begun.

Police officers, split into coordinated groups, moved methodically through the dense vegetation near Laxmipuram. Under the dimming sky, their torches flickered like scattered stars. Crickets had started chirping, and long shadows stretched between the trees. One team followed a trail that snaked past the old borewell; another advanced toward a dried canal, sweeping every patch of undergrowth.

Boots crunched over dead leaves. Walkie-talkies crackled with updates, the officers communicating in brief, sharp phrases.

But just as the operation settled into its rhythm, something unexpected — and violent — unfolded miles away.

A Kidnapping at the Tea Stall

It was just after 7:15 PM.

Ramesh, one of the five husbands of the missing mothers, stepped out from the police station. He had been inside all day — exhausted, questioning, waiting, hoping. Desperate for a breath of air and some tea, he crossed to the small roadside stall opposite the station.

The vendor, an elderly man with a white cloth wrapped around his head, served him a hot cup of chai. Ramesh lifted it to his lips.

That's when it happened.

A black van screeched to a halt beside them. No warning. No words.

Three masked men jumped out. They moved with violent precision. Before Ramesh could register what was happening, one swung a metal rod into his thigh. Another struck his back. He collapsed with a cry, the chai spilling across the pavement.

In seconds, he was thrown into the van.

And just as quickly — they were gone.

The Return of the Van

Fifteen minutes later, the black van returned — silent this time.

It pulled up at the same spot. The side door slid open.

Two of the masked men stepped out and dragged Ramesh's bloodied, semi-conscious body back onto the road like discarded trash. He hit the pavement with a dull thud. The van vanished once again, swallowed by the dark.

The tea vendor, trembling, ran to him and shouted for help.

"Somebody help! One of your men — he's dying!"

Police officers rushed from the station. They found
Ramesh barely able to move, bleeding from his back and
legs. Cuts, bruises, and swelling marred his body.

Pinned to his shirt pocket was a **deep red envelope**, edged
in gold. Just like the ones found earlier.

The Message Inside

Inside the station, the IPS officer was immediately
informed. Ramesh was rushed to a stretcher, doctors
summoned.

The envelope was handed over — unsealed, but
untouched. Its contents were crisp. Clean. Intentional.

It read:

"This is your first warning.
Stop searching the forest.
Withdraw your forces.
Or the next family member dies.
You've been warned."

The IPS read it twice. He said nothing at first. Then,
without emotion, he picked up the phone and dialled the
Senior Officer.

The Call That Changed Everything

"We've just recovered one of the husbands," the IPS said flatly. "He was abducted and beaten. There's a red envelope — a threat to stop searching."

A long silence.

Then the response came, quiet but resolute:

"You don't stop. You double it."

The IPS blinked. "Sir?"

"They want fear. Give them force."

The Senior Officer continued:

"Post immediate protection for all five families. Officers on every door. House lockdowns. But you — you go deeper. Mobilize weapons. Night teams. Enter farther into the forest. We don't back down."

"They touched one of ours. Now we finish this."

No Longer a Search — But a Stand

The IPS hung up.

His face didn't change, but his voice did.

He turned to his squad.

"Gear up. Bulletproof jackets. High-beam torches. Fully loaded rifles. We go back into the forest. This time, we don't walk quietly. We sweep."

Within minutes, weapons were checked. Radios recharged. Backpacks loaded.

As night descended fully over Laxmipuram, the second wave of police entered the woods — no longer searching passively. Now, they were ready to fight whatever darkness had dared to strike first.

The warning had been received.

But so had the message.

And the IPS officer's response was clear:

"We're not stopping."

Chapter 25: The Forest Takes Its Toll

Dusk in Laxmipuram

As darkness crept deeper over Laxmipuram, the forest began to change. What had earlier felt thick and mysterious now felt alive and hostile. Police torches cut through the gloom like narrow swords of light, flickering over trees that stood still and ancient like witnesses. The search was slow, deliberate — dozens of officers spread in all directions, forming concentric circles as they pressed deeper into the forest from multiple entry points. Their boots cracked on fallen twigs, radios whispered static, and the wind grew colder.

Suddenly, from the northeast sector, one officer saw
something strange — a soft, warm glow, far off through
the thick trees.

"There's light ahead!" he called out.

As others turned their torches in the direction, they could
all make it out — a light, possibly a fire or a lantern,
swaying gently in the woods.

Dozens of officers converged toward the glow, weaving
through thorny undergrowth and slippery stone. That was
when they reached it — a stretch of the river.

The River's Deception

The river water moved slowly at first, the sound barely
louder than a whisper. On one side of the bank, half the
officers stopped. On the other, the rest fanned out to cross.
The water was only ankle-deep and smooth — for now.

Midway through, as most of the officers carefully treaded
the riverbed, someone cried out —

"Water's rising!"

One officer stumbled. Another looked upstream — and
froze.

A towering wave of black water surged toward them —
silent at first, then roaring. The river, seemingly tame just

seconds before, turned monstrous. The wave crashed down like a wall, swallowing all mid-crossing. They vanished beneath the surface.

Screams rang out. The torches bobbed in the water. One by one, lights disappeared — until the entire crossing force was gone.

The Forest Reveals Its Cruelty

On the near bank, horror took hold. Officers called into their radios — but no response came back. Then, as they scanned the trees above them, their torches caught something — ropes. Five. Ten. Fifteen.

And then... bodies.

From the branches, lifeless uniformed figures began to appear — strung from the trees like broken marionettes. Faces bruised, eyes closed, some still clutching their rifles — it was the second half of their team.

They hadn't drowned. They had been hanged.

The lights from their helmets and flashlights lit the canopy above — revealing rope after rope, tied and thrown with terrifying precision.

The remaining officers screamed for help. Radios crackled. A last wave of men tried to retreat — but from the water, more bodies floated back toward the banks. Blood soaked through once-olive green uniforms.

By the time silence returned, over 60 officers had been wiped out.

The forest took them — violently, cruelly, and completely.

Echoes in the Canopy

The wind shifted. Leaves above the canopy rustled unnaturally, though no storm was present. The remaining officers on the safer bank were frozen, flashlights now shaking in their hands. Some lowered their beams out of instinct — not because they wanted to, but because they were afraid of what else they might see above.

One officer stepped backward, almost tripping over a gnarled root. Another shouted into his radio again, his voice trembling.

"This is team four— we've lost contact— river ambush— repeat, officers down! Officers…"

No reply.

All radios buzzed back nothing but static.

Then came another sound — soft at first, like wind rustling metal. But it wasn't wind. It was the rope — gently swaying under the weight of the dead.

One flashlight beam flicked upward again, and the horror was complete: one of the hanging bodies had a message pinned to their chest, flapping in the air. The officer nearest to the body tried to move forward, but his breath was caught in his throat.

Every instinct told him — this was no longer a rescue mission.

A Trap, not a Battle

One by one, remaining officers began to step back — but stepping back in a forest like Laxmipuram was dangerous. The undergrowth was thick. Roots twisted underfoot. Vision was narrow. And the sense of being watched was no longer just imagination.

Someone — something — had orchestrated this entire operation.

First, the bait of a glowing light in the woods. Then, the seemingly gentle river. Then, the wave. Then, the hangings. And finally, silence.

It was a trap — not improvised, but designed.

The Survivors and the Message

At the command post... From the edge of the forest, a senior officer tried once again to hail the ground units.

"Command to team. Do you copy?"

No answer.

Another officer beside him stared at the digital tracker board. All signals had gone dark.

One dot flickered faintly. Then blinked out.

"No signal from any squad," he whispered.

Then came a sound from the edge of the woods. Footsteps. A lone flashlight beam.

Two officers emerged — soaked, bruised, dragging a third between them who was unconscious and bleeding from his temple. They stumbled into the clearing.

"They're all gone…" one whispered. "They… the trees… the ropes… the water…"

One officer tried to explain, but his mouth was dry. He simply sank to the ground, eyes wide open, reliving every moment.

The IPS officer, who had rushed back after hearing silence from the teams, knelt beside the wounded man.

"What happened?" he asked quietly.

"They were waiting," the man whispered. "They… knew we'd come."

"Who?" the IPS asked.

"I don't know… but we were herded… we saw the light… it looked like help. But it wasn't."

He clutched the IPS's collar, his voice cracking.

"Sir... we didn't stand a chance."

Behind him, from the tree line, several bodies began to float back down the river. One after another.

The water now slow, gentle, deceptive. The same river that had taken them was now giving them back — lifeless.

The IPS stood slowly.

"No more search teams," he said. "For now."

"But this isn't over."

Chapter 26: The Call

A Stillness Too Deep

The forest was still. Too still.

After the massacre of his men, the IPS officer stood quietly near the command post, his boots soaked with mud and river spray, his eyes locked on the tree line. The smoke from flares hovered above, and the radio static around him was the only sound that dared to break the silence.

He had already begun giving orders to retreat. His voice was low, heavy, and reluctant. A hundred decisions buzzed in his mind — whether to pull back the teams entirely, regroup at district headquarters, or call for air support. The forest had won this round.

The Unexpected Ring

As he turned away from the wreckage, his phone rang.

The screen displayed a familiar name — Aryan's Father.

The IPS officer hesitated for just a moment. Then answered.

"Yes?" he said, his voice hoarse.

On the other end came the father's voice. Calm. Careful.

"Sir, Aryan wants to speak to you."

That sentence stopped the IPS officer in his tracks.

He stepped away from the few officers huddled behind him. His eyes narrowed. His heart beat a little faster.

"Put it on speaker," the IPS said, instinctively.

There was a brief pause, then the soft, steady voice of Aryan filled the line.

"Sir, under the bridge," Aryan said, "I have seen a car."

The IPS officer froze.

Aryan continued, "If you remember, I told you earlier — I saw it on Google Maps. It's near the Laxmipuram bridge."

The IPS officer said nothing. His hand gripped the phone tighter. His eyes were now staring into the black distance ahead.

"The colour... on the top," Aryan added. "Please check the Google Maps again. You'll see the car."

There was a silence that followed — only the soft hum of static and wind brushing through nearby trees.

The IPS opened his mouth, but no words came.

And then, as if it were the most natural thing in the world, Aryan added,

"Also, sir... can I have rose milk with cherry on the top?"

A Memory Rekindled

The IPS's breath caught.

"What...?"

Aryan's father could be heard faintly in the background. The IPS steadied himself and spoke again.

"Aryan, how do you know... Shankar Kaka's name?"

The boy didn't answer that. He only repeated, softly,

"I would like to come to your house, sir. Just for the rose milk. With the cherry on top."

The IPS's throat went dry.

He remembered clearly — that exact drink. Rose milk. Cherry. Prepared only by Shankar Kaka.

Only three people had ever asked for it: himself, his daughter, and her childhood friend — the daughter of his old friend, now gone.

His mind was racing. The timeline didn't match. Aryan was too young. He had never met this boy until the investigation. Yet, he spoke like he knew.

Like he remembered.

The IPS was no longer looking at the forest. He was staring into the distance, into memory, into something much older than the trees themselves.

"Go ahead," he whispered. "Go to the house. Shankar Kaka is waiting."

Aryan's father said, "Thank you, sir," and the call ended.

The Shift in the Forest

The IPS stood still for a long moment.

Behind him, the few surviving officers were tending to the wounded. One of them — his arm slung in a makeshift bandage, dried blood streaking down his cheek — walked up to him slowly.

"They're all gone, sir," the man said, voice flat. "The ones who crossed the river. The ones who stayed behind."

Another survivor approached — his uniform shredded at the shoulder. "It wasn't an ambush, sir," he said softly. "It was a plan. A message."

The IPS officer barely heard them.

In his mind, he wasn't in the forest anymore. He was back at his ancestral home — on the porch, with his daughter and her best friend, both laughing, sipping pink rose milk with cherries floating gently on top.

He had thought those memories were buried.

But Aryan's voice — calm, kind, and too familiar — had unearthed something that shouldn't have returned.

The IPS felt the back of his neck go cold.

He had come here chasing a mystery.

Now, he wasn't sure who was chasing whom.

Chapter 27: The Car Beneath the Bridge

A Memory in a Glass

The IPS officer sat down heavily on a nearby wooden bench that had been dragged near the command post. The weight of the past hour — the losses, the silence, the ghostly words from Aryan — bore down on him like an iron vest.

His mind wandered. Aryan's voice echoed in his ears again.

"Sir... can I have rose milk with cherry on the top?"

The words, so innocent and strange in the context of death and chaos, cut deeper than any bullet.

To him, that drink had never been a joke, never just a beverage. It was energy. Strength. His source of calm. A memory of a time long gone. Of moments spent at his best friend's house — the only place was, during their younger days, he could truly be himself. When the IPS was broken, exhausted, or lost, he didn't go to temples or shrines. He went to his friend's house — where the rose milk was made just right. With a cherry on top.

In his daydream, he could see it now — his younger self sitting in the veranda of the old house, his friend beside him sipping coffee, while two little girls — his daughter and her best friend — giggled under the shade of the mango tree, holding glasses of pink rose milk. The sun filtered through the branches. Everything was peaceful.

Then — a red rubber ball flew in from nowhere.

It hit the table, and their glasses tipped over. The rose milk spilled. The cherry bounced on the floor. He looked up sharply, startled — and the vision shattered like the glass it carried.

He was back in the present.

Back in the forest.

Surrounded by the stench of mud, sweat, and the thick air of dread.

Rose Milk and the Decision

He blinked. Looked around. Realized every officer was waiting — watching him. Waiting for him to speak. Waiting for orders.

He raised a hand.

"Get me rose milk," he said calmly.

There was a moment of absolute silence.

Then a rustle.

The driver sprinted to the vehicle, pulled out a stainless-steel container from the side storage box, and handed it to another constable. A moment later, a cup was filled and presented to the IPS.

He took the rose milk gently, almost reverently.

The cherry hadn't been added.

Without asking, the driver opened a smaller tin — where a few preserved cherries rested in syrup. He plucked one out and placed it on top of the pink froth, gently swirling it until it settled.

The IPS officer took the glass.

He closed his eyes as the first sip touched his lips. Cold. Sweet. Comforting.

But the cherry — it floated, brushing against his upper lip again and again. Each time it did, he pushed it back with his tongue, saving it for the last. Always for the last.

The officers watched in silence. This was not just a man drinking something. This was something else. Something sacred. Something old.

When he finally finished, he rolled the cherry into his mouth, crushed it between his teeth — and opened his eyes.

And then he said, "Get the crane. Or thick ropes. We're going to the bridge."

The Search Beneath

The men didn't ask questions. They moved.

The IPS walked slowly, pulling out his phone. Opening Google Maps. Zooming in. "Look," he said, showing the screen. "That... that's the car. Under the bridge. You see it?"

Everyone gathered around the screen. Yes. It was there — faint but clear. A shadowy shape in the water near the old Laxmipuram bridge.

Just then, the morning sun began to rise higher. The bridge, once cloaked in grey and fog, began to shimmer. A few beams of light broke through the trees and danced across the river.

The officers moved along the top of the bridge, squinting, scanning. They looked left, then right.

Nothing.

No car.

No reflection.

No sign.

The water had risen after the flash flood. It had become murky again. Fast-moving in some places. Still and deceptive in others.

"Where did the car go?" someone muttered.

The IPS was still chewing slowly — the cherry finally swallowed. He looked over the edge of the bridge and said, "Throw stones."

"What, sir?"

"Throw stones. Let's see if any sound different. A metallic sound."

The men obeyed. One by one, stones were tossed.

Each splash was the same — dull, wet, and hollow.

Until, finally — *clang!*

It was faint, but clear. A few feet downriver, a splash echoed with something sharper. Not water. Not mud.

"Again," he said.

Another stone. Another splash. *Clang.*

"There," he pointed. "There."

They moved quickly, but cautiously.

One officer shouted from downstream — "Sir! Something's there! Something white... metal...!"

Dozens rushed over.

There it was.

A **white car**, upside down, submerged in shallow water, the top barely visible, reflecting a pale glint in the morning light. Its sides dented. Its tires spinning slowly with the current.

No one dared to move closer.

The Recovery

"Sir," one constable said. "If another flood wave comes..."

The IPS didn't wait.

He removed his belt. Tied a rope around his waist. Took another long coil of rope in his hand.

And without another word — **jumped**.

He swam swiftly, powerfully, pushing against the water, reaching the car in less than a minute.

The entire team stood at the bank, holding their breath.

He tied ropes to the axle. The mirror. The frame.

The glass was still intact. No sign of movement inside.

He didn't break the glass. Not yet.

Let the car speak first.

"Pull!" he yelled.

And they did.

For three hours, using a crane, ropes, winches, and the combined muscle of two dozen men, they dragged the car inch by inch out of the river.

As the water sloshed off and the tires hit dry ground, silence fell again.

The **forensics team** approached. The **videographer** switched on his camera. Gloves were worn. Tools prepared.

Everyone gathered around.

The IPS officer wiped the sweat off his brow.

This was the moment.

They were going to open the car.

And find what — or **who** — waited inside.

Chapter 27: The Closure – The House That Wasn't There

The Car on the Riverbank

The car had finally been pulled to the riverbank. Water drained slowly from its broken frame, trickling back into the earth as if reluctant to release the secrets it held. Its white paint, now chipped and dulled by time, bore scratches as though the river had tried to keep it hidden for years. Bits of moss clung to its edges. A crow perched momentarily on its roof, cawed once, and flew away.

Silence fell over the gathered officers. No orders were given. No one moved.

The IPS officer stood a few feet away, arms behind his back, his boots planted firmly on the wet soil. Around him, the forensic team approached the vehicle with cutters, gloves, stretchers, and quiet prayers. They worked slowly, as if disturbing something sacred.

The driver's door creaked open first.

Inside were four bodies — or what was left of them. Skeletal remains, held together by worn seatbelts and collapsed upholstery. Two adult skeletons in the front seats. Two smaller ones in the back. The smaller skeletons had their arms entwined, as if they had clutched each other during their final moments.

Even the forensics team, hardened by years of field work, stepped back.

The IPS officer stepped forward alone.

This wasn't just any car.

He recognized it instantly. It had belonged to his dearest friend — the former Inspector General of the State, a man who had vanished one summer day years ago, his entire family with him. No trace had ever been found. No foul play confirmed. No closure given.

Until now.

His friend. His friend's wife. His daughter. And the daughter's best friend — the one who used to laugh beneath the mango tree. All here. All lost in silence.

The IPS officer did not cry. He had forgotten how.

But his chest rose once, sharply. His jaw tightened. He looked up at the trees, at the sun breaking over the canopy, and breathed in the morning air like it might restore something.

And then, he whispered, "Mobilize the team. We move now. There's light."

The House That Wasn't There

They moved like an army reborn.

Almost a hundred officers were dispatched, fanning out from the riverbank like a hive awakened. The command came from the IPS himself, and it was clear: this was not a rescue anymore. This was reclamation.

Boots pounded the soft ground. Radios snapped with clipped voices. Drones rose into the sky. The air smelled of dew, smoke, and justice.

Roughly two kilometre's in, through overgrown underbrush and tangled creepers, they found it.

A house.

A forgotten structure half-swallowed by the forest. Its roof sagged under moss and years of rain. Ivy draped over the broken windows. Wooden steps led to a porch eaten away by decay.

No nameplate. No path. No sign that it had ever existed.

And yet, there it was.

One officer whispered, "We passed this area last night. There was nothing here."

Another nodded in disbelief. "It wasn't here. I swear it."

But now, it stood quietly — as though it had always been there, just waiting to be seen.

The IPS officer arrived moments later.

He didn't pause. He didn't ask questions.

His boots touched the moss-laced steps. He raised his fist.

"Breach."

Chapter 28: The Closure – The Truth Beneath the Floor

The Ambush in the Forest

The forest had just started to warm under the mid-morning sun when the IPS officer, leading the charge toward the abandoned house, was suddenly hit.

A gunshot cracked through the silence. The bullet tore through his left shoulder.

He staggered but did not fall. His eyes, sharp and focused like a tiger, narrowed. Blood seeped through his uniform, but pain didn't slow him. It only sharpened his resolve.

He turned, scanning the treetops.

"Hide!" he barked to his men. "Scan the area. They're here. Look for ropes. Look for shadows."

The forest had eyes. Hidden assailants were perched among the branches. The IPS's instincts were right. Within moments, his team spotted two figures hiding in the trees.

"Fire!" he ordered.

Gunshots erupted.

A man fell from a tree, crashing onto the forest floor with a scream. Then chaos spread. Officers surged forward, spreading in every direction, chasing down figures emerging from the shadows. One by one, the gunmen were captured or killed. The ambush had been real — but the police were faster.

By the time the battle ended, the forest was under control.

The Encounter with Ravi

But the IPS officer, wounded but unrelenting, had already forced his way into the house.

Inside, in a dark, dusty hall, he met Ravi.

The art sir.

Ravi wasn't himself. His eyes wild, he swung a sword at the IPS without a word. A sharp slash cut across the IPS's side, but he fought back. Wounded but tactical, he dodged the next attack and waited. It was a trap.

Officers burst in through the windows. Ravi was overwhelmed and restrained.

Outside, some of the attackers lay dead. The rest were being interrogated. Ravi said nothing.

The Hidden Connection

Inside the abandoned house, a discovery was made. A stack of photographs.

Photos of the missing girls. Photos of Ravi and the coach — standing in the forest. Behind them, smiling students. The same day as the trip. But Ravi wasn't supposed to be there.

The IPS's suspicion grew. This was not random. It had been planned. Ravi and the coach were involved.

But someone else was behind it all.

Tracing the Coach

The IPS ordered men to go fetch the coach. They contacted the school — he hadn't come.

His house was locked.

They broke it open.

Inside was another shock. A photo. Laxmipuram temple entrance. A picture of the coach and Ravi.

The team informed the IPS, who ordered his men to move to the village temple.

Locals revealed the truth — the coach was a native of Laxmipuram. A house was identified. When the officers entered, they found him.

Hanging.

He had taken his life.

It was a blow.

Ravi still wouldn't speak. The whereabouts of the women remained a mystery.

The Key to the Bunker

But in the coach's house, they found another maroon envelope. Inside it: dollars. And an address. It was from the village sarpanch.

The IPS arrived at the coach's house. "We'll make Ravi speak," he said calmly.

Suddenly, a helicopter roared overhead.

The IPS turned to Ravi. "The coach is dead," he said.

Tears welled in Ravi's eyes.

"They're in the house," he whispered. "Below. A bunker. It's locked. The key... it was with him."

The team searched the coach's body again — and found the key. A thin chain around his neck.

The key was rushed to the IPS via helicopter.

Back at the house, they unlocked the bunker.

The Rescue

What they saw changed everything.

Over a hundred women and girls.

Alive.

Including the five missing women.

They were malnourished, terrified — but alive.

Helicopters were called in. One by one, the women were evacuated to the nearest hospital. Doctors stood ready. Vehicles lined the forest road.

And amid all this — Ravi, unattended, reached for a sharp metal object.

He stabbed himself.

By the time anyone noticed, it was too late.

He was gone.

The Final Fire

The IPS stood silent.

He wasn't finished.

He gathered a unit and rode to the house of the sarpanch.

The man was already waiting.

A tall figure, around 60, heavy gold chains on his chest, dressed in white. He stood at the door as though he'd expected them.

The officers advanced.

They smelled it before they saw it — petrol. Diesel.

The sarpanch stared them down.

"This is my town. You don't command me."

And then — fire.

He set himself ablaze.

The flames consumed him. And the house.

The police could do nothing but watch.

A final fire to hide the final truth.

But the girls were safe. The women were free. And the forest was no longer silent

Chapter 29: The Closure – Ashes and a Cherry

The Final Ritual

Three days later, the sacred ghats of the Ganga bore witness to a quiet, dignified ceremony.

The remains retrieved from the submerged car — the Inspector General, his wife, and their two children — had been placed in ceremonial urns. On the banks of the river, beneath a soft, overcast sky, rituals began.

The IPS officer, stripped of uniform and medals, stood in a plain white dhoti and shawl. His eyes, hollow yet resolved, stayed fixed on the river. Beside him, Aryan stood quietly — a boy who had seen more than his age should allow, holding steady beside the man who now carried the heaviest grief of all.

The River Takes Them Home

The priest chanted softly, his voice mingling with the hum of the wind and the lapping of the water. He lit the ceremonial lamp. The IPS stepped forward, holding the urn in both hands, his fingers trembling.

He lowered the ashes into the flowing Ganga, releasing them into the eternal current.

As he stepped back, a small cherry stem slipped from his robe and feel unnoticed into the water.

Unnoticed by all — except Aryan.

The boy watched it float, spin, and vanish downstream.

The wind stirred gently. The river rippled.

A Question Without an Answer

"Do you feel lighter now, sir?" Aryan asked softly.

The IPS didn't speak.

But he nodded.

The Last Drawing

As the wind moved across the ghats and the river carried away the ashes, something delicate glided with them — a single cherry, rolling calmly in the gentle current.

Beside the IPS, Aryan stood still.

In one hand, he held a drawing sheet — edges curled, charcoal lines still dark against the breeze.
In the other, a glass of rose milk, untouched, the cherry resting perfectly on top.

He did not drink.
He did not speak.
He simply watched.

The river.
The sky.
The moment.

A Story Carried Away

A sudden gust of wind swept through the ghats. The drawing sheet fluttered violently in Aryan's hand — and then, slipped free.

It flew across the breeze, tumbling lightly before settling on the surface of the river.

Aryan and the IPS both turned to watch as the paper floated downstream, slowly absorbing water. As it drifted, the lines of the sketch became visible — the image of a bridge, faintly drawn. A girl stood at its centre, facing the river, one hand raised as if waving. On the bank, a small figure — Aryan himself — stared back at her, tears streaking down his face.

The paper turned slowly in the current, spun once, then began to sink.

Aryan didn't move. The rose milk still untouched in his hand.

The IPS placed a hand gently on Aryan's shoulder.

They both watched the final piece of the story disappear beneath the ripples.

Contents

This story was not born from a single idea, but from a feeling — one that lingered quietly in the corners of the mind and refused to fade.

The Echoes on the bridge began with a simple question: What if a child's drawing revealed a truth that adults had long buried?

As the chapters unfolded, it became something more — a journey through memory, grief, innocence, and a mystery that stretches far beyond what is seen.

Through Aryan's eyes, I wanted to explore how the past returns — not always as punishment, but sometimes as unfinished truth. How a whisper from a river, a cherry in a glass of rose milk, or a shadow beside a bridge could carry more weight than words.

This is not just a story of a missing car or five vanished girls.

It is a story about silence — and how, in the right hands, silence becomes a map.
It is about memory — and how children sometimes see what truth itself hides.
It is about the ache of unresolved love, and the strength of stillness.

The Echoes on the bridge is just the beginning — the first part of a larger journey.

I hope it makes you pause.
I hope it makes you wonder.
And most of all, I hope it stays with you.

Rakesh Kumar Bhavani
(Author)

Acknowledgements

To my better half, Annapurna, and my sons, Aryan and Akash — you are the light that guides me, even when the pages turn dark.

To my father, Damodar, for his quiet strength and belief in me.

And to my beloved mother, Sharadha — though you are no longer with us, your warmth, grace, and love live on in every word of this story. This book is a tribute to your memory.

Prologue

Years ago...

The forest was quiet that morning — unnaturally so.

Not even the birds dared to sing. Only the sound of leaves crackling under footsteps. A car — white, old, slow — turned off the narrow road and rolled toward the bridge. Four passengers. Two in the front. Two in the back.

The man driving looked over his shoulder one last time. "Are we doing the right thing?" he asked.

His wife didn't answer.

In the backseat, two children pressed their faces to the window, watching the river shimmer as it moved under the bridge. The world didn't know what was about to disappear.

And the river — calm and cruel — kept flowing

To Those Who Walked With Me

To my better half, Annapurna, and my sons, Aryan and Akash — you are the light that guides me, even when the pages turn dark.

To my father, Damodar, for his quiet strength and belief in me.

And to my beloved mother, Sharadha — though you are no longer with us, your warmth, grace, and love live on in every word of this story. This book is a tribute to your memory